M000039273

A LONE RED APPLE

A NOVEL

BY AURELIA

For Julia Anasoulis
Enjoy this Valentine
to Greece!
Aurelia 2001

Greek America Press

Established 1998
406 Wimer Drive
Pittsburgh, Pennsylvania 15237

Copyright © 1997 by Aurelia Smeltz
All rights reserved
Published in the United States by Greek America Press

LIBRARY OF CONGRESS CATALOGING IN PUBLICATION DATA
A Lone Red Apple: a novel/Aurelia.—1st edition

ISBN: 1-892430-00-2
LCCN: 98-96215
First Edition 1998

Design and typography by Jill Goodmon
Set in Baker Signet and Herculanum

Illustrated by Bill Papas

Printed in the United States of America

DEDICATED TO:

μεν
On the one hand...

Sappho

My inspiration.
Long, long ago she said:
"My words shall live forever."

δε
And on the other hand...

My Husband, Jack

My guide and companion
in a delightful journey
through literature
and life.

ACKNOWLEDGMENTS

THE MUSES.

My husband, Jack; my Greek friend and mentor, Gregory C. Pappas; and my British friend and mentor, Gerald Burke. This book would not have been written without my husband's enthusiasm and guidance; Gregory Pappas' affection for this story and his infectious passion for Greece; and Gerald Burke's elegant British ways and equally elegant editorial suggestions.

THE THREE GRACES.

My story was enriched by Three Graces, who are my very special friends, Aleka Angeletaki, Dr. Cornelia Davis, and Ellen McLean. All three read and re-read my manuscript in the early stages and offered reactions, suggestions, and constant encouragement.

THE ORACLE.

Dr. Albert C. Labriola, a master teacher and my friend, revealed to me the secrets of understanding and interpreting great literature.

THE CHORUS.

A chorus of kind people helped, either by encouraging me or by generously providing me with information from their special fields. They are: Stella Athanasiou, Rick and Edith Benzinger, Georgia Blotzer, Dr. Marianne Bouvier, Robert and Diana Bowden, Lonnie Barton, George Chryssis, Dr. Jerry Clack, Kallirroi Deligianni, Rina Ferrarelli, Donna Gertz, John Hanes, Dr. Lorna Hardwick, Doree Horn, Bruce Krane, Charlie Kyriacou, Michael and Lisa Labriola, Marina Nash, Foster Provost, Cindy Pope, Sara Ruck, Sam Sandora, Dina Skias, Bill Warren, and Dr. Ann Wilkins.

THE ARTIST.

Bill Papas, a creative genius and artist of international renown, designed the cover and illustrated this book. He turned a simple love story into a work of art.

THE TRANSLATORS.

As you will discover as you read this story, Sappho's poems were translated by the students of Matthew Wyttman!!!

◤◤◤

Special thanks to Denise Sylvester Carr, who edited the sections on Greenwich and Blackheath and provided me with historical information; and to Susan Wadsworth Booth, who edited the entire manuscript in a masterful way.

Special thanks, also, to my friend and colleague, Brandon Wilson, who handled all administrative details and offered constant support.

I am most grateful to Bill and Maria Warren and to the owners of the Hotel Akrogiali for their hospitality during my two summers on Mykonos, and to Beryl and Fred Mason, who provided me with lovely accommodations, including the garden where I wrote part of this manuscript, in Greenwich. Thanks to Beryl, also, for conducting research and for taking photographs.

A LONE RED APPLE

The gods of Olympus sit serenely on their thrones as a dignified procession of citizens parades before them. Some Athenians are on foot, others ride in chariots, and a few sit proudly on handsome horses. Accompanied by musicians holding flutes delicately to their lips, the nubile maidens and athletic young men, noble soldiers, proud dignitaries, and assorted attendants, carrying olive branches and trays of ambrosia, float by as in a dream. On the shoulders of some girls are jugs of wine and nectar, while older women carry in their hands a garment they have woven for the virgin goddess, Athena. She, the patroness of Athens, is seen nearby rising full-born from the head of Zeus. With her slender hands extended in a gesture of welcome, she offers her city and its gracious hospitality to the Olympian gods.

The pageant leaves him breathless, as it always has. The fact that he has seen it many times before does not take anything away from its timeless splendor. This parade of the meek and mighty paying homage to the gods captures the grandeur, the spirit, and the very soul of the golden age. The glory that was Greece is there for all to see.

"Look carefully," Matthew Wyttman says to the students now surrounding him in the Acropolis Museum and straining to see minute details on the sculptures. He wants them to observe that the depth created by the artist makes it appear that the horses and chariots are about to pass each other.

He is explaining the fine points of the friezes to his six students, Jim, Brandon, Christos, and Kallirroi from America, and James and Dina from Britain.

They are examining a reproduction of the most famous frieze from the Parthenon, the ancient temple that crowns the Acropolis. Matthew devotes most of his attention to this sculpture before directing the students' attention to others, explaining their unique characteristics. Pointing, he says, "on this particular frieze we see Athena again, but this time she is at war with Poseidon."

"The god of the sea," Jim says.

"Yes," the professor acknowledges, "and even though this is a reproduction, the details are clear."

"Where on the Parthenon were these particular friezes located?" James asks.

"Poseidon and Athena were depicted on the west pediment of the temple, and on the east was the glorious birth of the virgin goddess.

"The Parthenon is now over 2,000 years old and is the greatest monument to the gods in western civilization," Matthew explains.

"I saw the light and sound show here last night," Kallirroi offers. "The Parthenon looked very different with all the colored lights shining on it."

"We are accustomed to a white Parthenon, but it was not always white; some parts of it were painted rather gaudily in bright hues of blue and red and perhaps yellow," Matthew explains, to the amazement of the students. "But at least they stayed with primary colors," he adds.

He continues, "At one time there were 92 distinctive friezes on this temple, and the scenes covered 525 feet. The friezes were within the portico, along the outer wall."

"Where are they now?" Christos asks.

"The majority of the originals are in The British Museum where they were taken by Lord Elgin," Matthew explains.

"They're called The Elgin Marbles," Dina offers.

"Yes, Dina," Matthew says, looking over the top of his glasses, "they are called that, but they really are The Parthenon Marbles. As you know, the fact that they were taken from Greece is still very controversial, and we will talk more about this later. Some are in the Louvre in Paris, others are in museums here, and still others can be seen in their original positions on the Parthenon where they were over 2,000 years ago. Just imagine that."

"But look! the temple is so high; the Doric columns appear to touch the clouds," Brandon interjects, pointing to the Parthenon above them. "How can anyone see the friezes? How could the ancients see the full glory of what was being depicted?"

"They could not," Matthew responds, "but perhaps they were not meant to see it. Perhaps it was intended for the enjoyment of the gods alone!!"

Putting his materials in his briefcase, and removing his glasses as he says this, he indicates that the lecture is over. There is still much to see, however, and he and the students linger for some time in the Acropolis Museum, studying reproductions of the friezes from the Parthenon. This is their final stop in Athens before beginning the journey to the sacred island.

瑞瑞瑞

As they leave the museum, the heat of the day is almost suffocating. The temperature is over 110 degrees Fahrenheit. Soon cars and mopeds are everywhere, speeding about, and the pollution is heavy. Matthew is glad he made the decision to leave the next day from the small port of Rafina, rather than from the international hub of Piraeus. "Piraeus will be sizzling," he thinks.

That decision alone sets Matthew Wyttman apart from most foreigners in Greece traveling to the outer islands. It is mainly Greeks who know about Rafina and choose to leave from there.

The students tell Matthew they plan to spend their last night in Athens in the Plaka section and also in Syntagma Square. They say they will be in the lobby of the Athenian Inn early tomorrow afternoon, ready to leave with him for the bus stop at Areos Park and the one-hour ride to Rafina.

"Walk gingerly through the traffic, and beware of the mopeds," Matthew tells them as he departs, looking once again to the top of the Acropolis at the Parthenon and bowing his head slightly, a deferential farewell to this magnificent temple of the Olympian gods.

瑞瑞瑞

Arriving on the west coast of Attica in plenty of time, the students decide not to stroll around Rafina's main square, but to board the boat as soon as possible. Matthew, on the other hand, lingers on the pier and is one of the last to board.

Before his first visit here, a Greek friend advised him to leave for Mykonos from Rafina and to book passage on the *Penelope*, the big ferryboat that carries passengers, freight, and automobiles. Matthew found this to be excellent advice. This ship travels 71 nautical miles and makes two stops, one at Andros and the other at Tinos, before reaching Mykonos. Boats leaving Piraeus traverse 94 nautical miles to reach the same destination.

A bustling port for luxury liners and commercial traffic from all over the world, Piraeus is one of the best known and busiest ports in the Mediterranean. Rafina, on the other hand, is a small and charming village where fishermen sell their catch directly from their boats to the cooks in the tavernas. In fact, before boarding the ferry, Matthew selects a red mullet from a bed of ice in a glass case and goes into the taverna's kitchen to watch the cook expertly sprinkle the fish with olive oil and fresh herbs, stuff it with lemon slices, and then grill it to perfection.

In contrast to the rapid hydrofoils, with their rigid rows of metal seats, narrow aisles, and television sets every twenty feet, the *Penelope* is spacious, stately, and serene, with an old-world ambience. It features a dozen well-appointed private staterooms, coveted by travelers, but assigned at the captain's discretion, and two levels of commodious dining rooms and bars with well-worn mahogany tables and once-elegant upholstered chairs, arranged in erratic patterns.

The students find seats on the upper level and Matthew, wanting to give them privacy, chooses the lower deck. On both levels, soft music lulls voyagers into relaxation as the vessel gently rocks over the rough sea, taming the waves by its size.

Today, this large freighter is unusually crowded. Because of a choppy sea, caused by winds that registered a high 8 on the Beaufort scale, the sleek hydrofoils scheduled to leave that morning for Mykonos and arrive in less than three hours had been canceled. Passengers who had morning reservations on these rapid vessels, the *Sea Jet* and the *Delphini*, are now on the *Penelope*, and most are not happy. This huge vessel leaves the port shortly after 5 p.m., lumbering steadily along on the rolling waves. It will take four hours or more for the ship to reach the northeast corner of the "white islands" of the Cyclades, where Mykonos, known as "The Venice of Greece," sparkles as a chalk-colored precious stone, a jewel of the Aegean.

Matthew and the students will stay on this island and take another boat, weather permitting, to and from the sacred island of Delos for the seminar. It is a short, twenty-minute trip, but on it they will see magnificent, deep vistas of the sea.

Passengers on the *Penelope* pass the time in a variety of ways. Seasoned travelers simply relax, take brief naps, or read. But first-time voyagers, such as the students, are understandably excited and want to talk about the islands and the adventures that lie ahead.

Several of the students are having a lively conversation with three Greek men considerably older than they. The men, retired seafarers, speak fluent English.

"You seem to know a great deal about the seaports and the sea," Dina declares.

"We spent our lives on freighters," Stephanos explains. "You have probably seen them flying the blue and white flags.

"With my two friends here, Petros and Nikolaos, we traveled up and down every inch of Greece's coast line, the longest in Europe."

"We sailed to the west in the Ionian Sea and to the east in the Aegean," Petros says.

"And to the South in the moody Mediterranean," Nikolaos interjects.

"Fascinating," James says. "Are you going sailing on the islands?"

"No," Petros responds, "we are just going home. We were in Athens visiting our relatives. We almost didn't know them. They wear suits now."

Kallirroi is anxious to learn more about this new land she is visiting and asks, "How many islands are there in all of Greece?"

"One estimate says thousands, but not all are inhabited, and some of them may be just big rocks," Nikolaos explains, adding that people probably live on about 120 of the islands.

"On a few of them you will find only old monks; on others, just shipping billionaires and their families; on still others, a few shepherds with their sheep and goats," Stephanos adds.

"What brings you young people to Greece?" asks Petros.

"We are here for a seminar," James says. "It will be taught on the island of Delos, but we will be staying on Mykonos."

"Will you be learning about the gods and the journey of Odysseus?" Petros asks.

"Not during this seminar," James says. "We are here to study lyric poetry. We read Homer's *Odyssey* last semester."

"Ah, the great epic," Petros says. "And tell me, what great lesson did you learn?"

"There were many lessons to be learned," James says, somewhat defensively.

"True, true," Stephanos interjects, "but I agree with my friend, there is one great lesson to be learned."

"Won't you tell us what it is?" asks Christos.

"Yes, tell us," pleads Jim.

"It is no mystery," Petros says, "and it is as true today as it was thousands of years ago.

"Perhaps when your visit to Greece is over you will know the answer as well as I do, but I will tell you.

"The lesson of *The Odyssey* is that one must respect the gods and acknowledge their power," Petros finally reveals, as Matthew walks past, heading for the upper deck. Hearing this, Matthew smiles and nods his approval.

"Ah, but you are serious students, you must know already that this is the great lesson of *The Odyssey*," Nikolaos says.

"Yes, but I have never heard that theme expressed as clearly as you have explained it," Jim says.

"That, my young man," Petros says, "is because I am Greek; I am of the sea. I know firsthand about respecting and acknowledging the power of the gods."

Unlike his students, Matthew Wyttman is a seasoned traveler who prefers to simply read and relax during the journey. He enjoys the leisurely pace of the *Penelope*, his vessel of choice for his past six trips to the islands.

Matthew is a lecturer at a London university, where he teaches subjects in the ancients, including classical Greek lyric poetry. His salary is modest, but he applied for and earned a faculty grant this year to teach this seminar. He negotiated a special price for his accommodations on Mykonos and visited a number of travel agencies on King's Road to find a charter flight cancellation, "flight only, without villa." These bargains are offered on a last minute basis, so Matthew was able to get a round trip from Heathrow to Athens at less than half fare.

Matthew's major scholarly endeavor is translating Greek manuscripts. A loner, set in his ways, his specialized knowledge keeps most people at a distance. The exception to this is Claire Billington, Head of the Classics Department, who is very much attracted to Matthew. This creates a problem and requires delicacy. While he has no romantic interest in Claire, Matthew does need her support for promotion to the Senior Lectureship that he covets.

At 40, tall and thin with eyes and hair varied shades of brown, Matthew is handsome. His ruddy complexion, warm brown hair, and rustic clothing remind one of autumn. He projects a relaxed, calm demeanor true to the scholar he is. Fluent in ancient and modern Greek, he is traveling to the islands once again to teach a seminar on lyric poetry. This year, he will teach the poetry of Sappho, Greece's most famous lyric poet, known as "The Tenth Muse." But he does not plan to conduct the seminar on Mykonos, where tourists come to sunbathe in the nude on beaches called "Paradise" and "Super Paradise," and then dance until dawn at discos that open at 11 p.m. and close at 7 a.m. He will teach this year where he taught before, on the sacred island of Delos, six nautical miles southwest of Mykonos in the Aegean.

According to Greek mythology, Apollo—god of music and light and son of Zeus—was born on Delos. It was once the religious center for ancient Greece and a busy trade port of the Mediterranean world. This island is designated by the Greek government as a protected archeological site, and no one is allowed to live there or remain overnight. Tourists may visit the ruins on Delos, however, and scholars are permitted to teach there, with special permission. Matthew plans to teach his seminar at either the Archaeological Museum or The Great Temple of Apollo.

൭൭൭

If Matthew relishes his leisurely journey on the *Penelope*, Elena does not. If she had left on the Sea Jet at 8:00 that morning as she had planned, she would be at her destination by now. She is anxious to return to her small studio apartment by the windmills on Mykonos, the island of her birth, after spending several months in Athens negotiating with various galleries to sell her watercolors. Elena looks forward to this summer and envisions the scenes she has been commissioned to paint and then sell when she returns to Athens. By her side is a watercolor of four windmills, historic landmarks on Mykonos. She is most pleased with her latest rendering of this scene and concentrates intently on images for future paintings, trying unsuccessfully to block thoughts of family troubles from her mind.

A slim and graceful 26-year-old, Elena has lovely dark hair and eyes that are a stark contrast to the incredible light that bathes the Greek islands. Her looks are dramatic; she reminds one of the vivid colors of summer. She has friends, but she is selective and prefers spending much of her time alone. She treasures her solitude and is a serious student of Hatha yoga, as practiced by the great master, Iyengar. Striving to achieve a balance of body and mind, Elena practices a variety of intricate postures or "asanas" at dawn on secluded beaches.

Elena enjoys wearing loose-fitting clothing that gives merely a hint of her perfect figure, and she affects a saucy, leave-me-alone attitude. Her attire and demeanor mask her fine qualities to all but the discerning eye.

There is a sadness in this young woman. Only those closest to her know she is alienated from her parents, Tassos and Katerina Angelides, who live on Mykonos with her older brother, Yiorgos. They are embarrassed by Elena's bohemian ways and feel she is ruining her life. They want her to come to them for advice, but she does not. They resent the fact that she considers herself cosmopolitan because of the two years she spent in the United States.

She lived with American cousins in Joliet, Illinois, who sponsored her while she attended an art institute during the day and worked in their restaurant at night to pay her way through school. The Greek community there descends from ancestors who emigrated from Mykonos to work as "gandy dancers," skilled workmen who laid track for the new railroad. Even though Elena had relatives there, her parents objected to her leaving home and living so far away in distant America. These are just some of many problems between Elena and her parents. There are things that cannot be spoken.

Though Elena and her family are not totally estranged, they remain aloof from each other. In retaliation for what the elder Angelides' see as unacceptable behavior, they sometimes use a few English words when speaking to her and call her "Helen." They do this to irritate her because she seemed to enjoy living in America against their wishes. She would like to reconcile with her family, but does not know how. So she remains a free spirit, practicing yoga, riding her moped, and enjoying Greek dancing while at home.

Matthew and Elena pass each other several times in *Penelope*'s dining room, but she hardly notices him. Elena hears Matthew's distinctive British accent as he talks with another passenger and notices that he appears reserved. She pays little attention initially, but the second time she hears his voice she is surprised and looks toward him as he speaks.

"Θα μπορουσα να εχω ενα χυμο πορτοκαλι παρακαλω; (May I have some orange juice, please?) Με παγακια;" (With ice?), Matthew asks the barmaid in fluent Greek, with a British accent.

He slips his eyeglasses down on his nose when he speaks and looks over them as he talks to her.

"Ευχαριστω πολυ" (Thank you very much), Matthew says, accepting the juice and smiling broadly.

"Παρακαλω" (You are welcome).

Elena notes that his Greek is flawless, and she likes his smile as well. He has a slightly rumpled look with his wrinkled clothing and disheveled hair. He looks like a big, bashful boy, she thinks. Elena has just ordered coffee and is seated near the bar at a corner table, carefully sketching a picture from a photograph. The waitress sets the coffee before her, commenting, "What a handsome boy you are sketching. Such a mop of curly black hair!!"

"My precious godson, Nikos," Elena says, "only five years old."

She looks up to see that Matthew is looking over his glasses and has now noticed her. As her eyes meet his, he runs his fingers through his hair, trying to make it neater. Lowering her gaze, she concentrates again on her sketch, brushing the long black hair covering her face back over her ear. Matthew observes that her profile is perfect. He thinks that if her eyes were gray, she would look exactly like his image of the goddess Athena. But her eyes are deep and dark and very brown.

ᄅᄅᄅ

Zeus, the supreme god, is bored and has directed his wife, Hera, to summon a goddess to cause some mischief among mortals for his entertainment. "Awaken a goddess from her ancient sleep," Zeus directs. Hera ponders his request, considers his mood, and then chooses Aphrodite, goddess of love and beauty.

Unfolding like a rose petal from a long rest and laughing sweetly, Aphrodite says she will entertain Zeus, but she wants the company of her servant, Eros, and the poet, Sappho. Intrigued, Hera agrees and sprinkles them with dew to end their sleeps.

High in the clouds, Aphrodite is now awake, her violet-hued mantle still covering her and Eros. Next, the poet Sappho stirs, her lyre by her side.

Aphrodite is the irresistible goddess; neither men nor gods can escape her charms. Some say she is the daughter of Zeus and Dione, but others insist she sprang full born from the foam of the sea near Cytherea. She has been immortalized by poets as "Violet-crowned Cytherea," but her name, Aphrodite, is from the Greek word "αφρος" (aphros), and it means foam.

Aphrodite is circled by radiance and sometimes appears as a brilliant flash of light. She creates beauty and happiness. Sometimes when she appears, green fields are suddenly covered with brilliantly colored flowers and the waves of the sea have been known to laugh.

Eros, the god of love, is Aphrodite's faithful servant. He is a beautiful young man immortalized by the philosopher, Plato, who said, "Love—Eros—makes his home in men's hearts, but not in every heart, for where there is darkness, he departs." Eros is often depicted with his bow and arrow, and his Latin name is Cupid. He serves Aphrodite and fulfills her wishes.

Sappho, though not a goddess, is the greatest lyric poet of Greek antiquity who predicted "my words will live forever." She lived on the island of Lesbos around the turn of the seventh and sixth centuries B.C. and wrote nine books of poetry, none of which *remain. After her death, other poets called her "the Tenth Muse," in recognition of her memorable lyrics.*

Aphrodite, Sappho, and Eros are now awake as dusk descends and the Penelope approaches the harbor of Mykonos. Sappho and Aphrodite gleefully conspire, as Eros stands in waiting, bow and arrow ready. Tonight they will enter the lives of two mortals. Which unsuspecting humans will they choose?

Matthew ventures onto the deck, carrying one suitcase and a book of Sappho's poems. He finds it thrilling to arrive at Mykonos at night and see hundreds of lights dancing through the bleached white village. Elena, carrying her portfolio, joins other passengers on the deck. She savors the view. To her artist's eye, the town looks like a gigantic sculpture embraced by rugged hills.

Matthew's thoughts are on his seminar and his translation project. He is very focused, and now that he is away from the distractions of the city and the university, he plans to accomplish much. Elena's thoughts are troubling. She mulls over the problems with her family. It is still early evening, and she will go and see them tonight. She has been in Athens for two months. Perhaps their attitudes have softened. At least they will not argue about the controversial plans to build a new marina and airport in the town, because these plans have been delayed. For such a major expansion, approval is needed from the government in Athens and this may take a year or more.

The book of poetry and the watercolor of the windmills intrigue the Olympian creatures. They watch as the mortals holding these objects cast approving glances at each other! Without a pause, they choose the mortals Matthew and Elena for their mischievous games. "We will have to get to know them better," Sappho says. "Of course, of course," the goddess of love agrees.

After the boat docks, Matthew, who is now with the students and far behind Elena as they disembark, is close enough to see a young man approach her. His black trousers and a white shirt have the look of a uniform. Matthew observes that Elena is annoyed with the man and moves quickly away. Matthew hears him shout:

"Πως μπορεις να ξεχασεις τοσο γρηγορα, Ελενα; (How can you forget so quickly, Elena?)

"Θα σε δω σε λιγο, Ελενα, Η Μυκονος ειναι μικρο νησι!!" (I'll see you soon, Elena. Mykonos is a small place!!)

Elena and her family live near each other, in fact within walking distance. Her mother and father own their home. It is in a narrow passageway, a bit sheltered from pedestrian traffic. Elena's studio apartment has a lovely view of the sea.

Small craft shops are nearby, but the Angelides family and their neighbors have somehow managed to prevent craft and clothing shops from opening on their "street." Tourists do their shopping on the other side of the quay where the exclusive stores of the gold merchants await them as they first set foot on the island.

Mykonos is noted for its gold merchants. Passengers from the cruise ships flock to purchase the unique and expensive handcrafted jewelry for which the island is famous. Owners and salesmen stand outside their shops, politely and charmingly inviting the tourists inside to see their exquisite designs. Customers are expected to bargain before a final price is agreed upon, and, for the merchants, astute bargaining is part of the thrill of the sale.

By ordinance, all the homes in Mykonos, and the stepping stones between them, must be painted white. Splashes of color are allowed on the shutters that protect the small windows, but these are usually red, blue, green, or brown. To add to the charm of this Cycladic island, all homes and buildings in the town are arranged in a maze, and there are no street signs or numbers on the houses.

Domes and crosses from the many churches, and paddles atop the famous windmills, jut diagonally as dramatic contrasts to the cube-shaped, sparkling clean white houses and shops. Painters and sculptors adore Mykonos Town.

In the family home, Elena's parents and her brother, Yiorgos, sit around the kitchen table discussing the local news and gossip, eating platters of fresh tomatoes, kalamata olives, and cucumbers sprinkled with olive oil and dotted with fresh feta cheese. Thick slices of bread, cut from a round loaf, are passed around. Little Nikos has been put to bed.

In the early evenings in Mykonos Town, the doors to family homes are usually not locked. Elena enters, saying, "Καλησπερα, Καλησπερα."

Her mother, Katerina, repeats Elena's greeting, but speaks in English. ("Good evening, good evening. Come in, Helen.")

This response in English is like a slap to Elena, but she is determined to try to communicate. (After making her point, Elena's mother and the other family members speak to Elena in Greek.) They ask her to join them at their meal and she does, but the conversation is stilted.

PAN   SAPPHO   APHRODITE

Katerina busies herself slicing tomatoes and cucumbers, and Elena's father concentrates on his meal, eating in silence. Yiorgos attempts to make conversation with Elena.

"How was Athens?" he asks.

"Hot as usual. Unbearably hot. And the traffic congestion is getting worse," Elena responds.

"All the more reason to stay in Mykonos," Yiorgos says.

"Yes, all the more reason to stay in Mykonos," Katerina agrees.

Elena sighs and tries one more time.

"They are trying to solve the problem of pollution from the automobiles. Only cars with even numbers on the ends of their license plates are allowed in Athens on certain days, and those with odd numbers on other days," she explains.

"Ha!" says Yiorgos, "I would like to see them trying to enforce that rule!"

"I hear some rich people get around this rule by buying a second car with alternate numbers on the plates," Elena says, straining now to make conversation.

"We don't have that problem with traffic and license plates in Mykonos," Katerina says.

The effort to start a conversation makes Elena weary, and she says she is tired and must go.

"Is Nikos asleep?" she asks.

"Yes," Katerina answers, "but come and see him tomorrow morning."

"I will try. If not tomorrow, the next day for sure," Elena says, "but I have things to do tomorrow."

"Of course, of course," her mother says.

As she gets up to leave, her mother says, in English, "Goodnight, Helen."

"Καληνυχτα!!" Elena says, defiantly.

When Elena leaves, her mother says, "She has things to do! What? How does she spend her time? How does she spend her time?"

▨▨▨

Alone. Elena spends most of her time alone, especially in the early mornings. This is her favorite time of the day. Usually, she walks in splendid solitude as Dawn spreads her rosy fingers over the blue/green waters of the Aegean Sea and the sparkling, sun-bleached sands of a secluded beach far from the hotels. Elena never walks near the hotels and sometimes climbs over hills to avoid that long stretch of prime beach property. Yannis, the young man who had approached her as she disembarked from the boat, works in a beach hotel, and she always tries to avoid him. And there are other, more significant, reasons why Elena dislikes that area.

On this June morning, Elena savors the cool, sea-kissed breezes at her favorite beach. She is preparing to do her yoga. She calls this simply her "practice" or her *asanas*. She does this only when she is at peace with herself or deeply troubled. There is seldom an in-between. This morning she feels at peace.

Elena feels confident that decisions she has made recently are correct. It is painful for her to think of her past, and yet she does not know how to share her present life. How can she dream of a future? The present is all she has.

Sappho and Aphrodite watch from above, studying the young woman. "Look, Aphrodite, how she blends in and is one with nature. She is a Sister to the Dawn."

Walking with a sense of purpose, Elena begins to discard her baggy outer clothing and, throwing back her head and her arms in a gesture of greeting, she faces the rosy Dawn, wearing a simple white exercise garment. She takes the barrette from her hair and the raven-colored silken strands cascade to her waist. Elena then stands almost motionless. An observer would not be aware that she is carefully aligning her body and trying to find the center of her balance before beginning her practice. She always strives to find this center, this balance, but is not convinced she has found it as yet. When she feels her body is properly aligned, she executes a regime of intricate *asanas*, slowly, effortlessly, and with lyrical grace. She ends her practice with a graceful backbend, and, as she comes up, she once again salutes the Dawn, whose rose-tipped fingers are now spread in a caress over the island.

Elena has thoroughly enjoyed her Mykonos morning. She is already looking forward to her Mykonos night, her first since returning to the island.

"Aphrodite," Sappho says, "I honored Dawn by giving her golden sandals. Elena honors her with graceful gestures. She must be a dancer." "Oh no," Aphrodite says, "remember the painting of the windmills? She is a painter, here to paint scenes of Mykonos." "Interesting," Sappho muses, "she will be painting on Mykonos, but Matthew is teaching on Delos. Hmmm!"

⌐⌐⌐

E lena rides her moped into town and stops on the quay to get a cup of strong, Greek coffee and read the local newspaper. Men and women, fellow Mykoniates, are gathered by the newspaper stand, talking and gesturing in a very animated fashion. They are talking about the marina and the airport. She quickly orders her coffee and then buys one of the local newspapers. The headline reads:

NEW MARINA AND AIRPORT
WILL BRING PROSPERITY

The front page story explains that approval is expected from the government to proceed with the expansion plans. Developers will begin making offers to persons who own homes where the marina is to be built. Elena quickly goes back to the newsstand to purchase another paper. Since the controversy began over development plans, those opposing the scheme began publishing their own newspaper. Elena has friends within this group and supports their efforts to stop expansion of the marina. Their headline reads:

THREE HISTORIC WINDMILLS
TO BE DESTROYED BY PROGRESS

The facts in this story are essentially the same, but the point of view differs. The story explains that if the people who own land where the marina is to be expanded agree to sell, the windmills, which are not only historic landmarks but distinctive symbols for the island, will be destroyed.

Elena is perplexed. She thought this issue was dormant for the time being. It was supposed to rest until a hearing was held in Athens. What could have happened? This means that the arguments with her family will begin again. Their home is near the windmills, and they have made it clear to Elena that they want to sell.

Far from the secluded spot where Elena completed her practice, Matthew is unpacking in his comfortable studio apartment at the Hotel Nissaki, perched on a cliff over-looking Platys Yalos Beach. The hotel is on the quiet part of a bay, far from the bars and lively discos, and he has an excellent view of the sea glittering in the rays of the sun. The two female students are sharing a room in a nearby hotel, and the young men have chosen to stay at the beautiful campsites scattered about the island.

When he steps onto his balcony, Matthew is soothed by the cool sea breezes. In the harbor, he can see the small boats that whisk tourists to "Paradise" and similar sunning places. Matthew had visited these beaches once, but never returned. Beaches with nude sun bathers are not to his liking.

In London, Matthew spends some mornings walking slowly near his home in Greenwich Park visiting the Old Royal Observatory. There he stands on the meridian line, straddling two hemispheres, surveying the peaceful beauty of the park. On most mornings, though, Matthew is in the British Library concentrating on his manuscripts. He transcribes texts in the original Greek language and then translates these texts into modern English. He also teaches ancient Greek literature to undergraduates who read the classics at university. The course he enjoys teaching most is the poetry of the legendary Sappho.

Matthew's first love is ancient documents. He does his research in The Round Reading Room of The British Library and enjoys camaraderie with other scholars who stay at the nearby William Goodenough House. One must have a reader's pass issued by the Library to use the famed room, built in 1857 and called by some "the most literary and scholarly spot in the world." It is where W.B. Yeats, T.S. Eliot, Oscar Wilde, and Karl Marx studied and wrote. A copper dome, supported by twenty cast iron ribs, soars over the book-lined room where desks and other reading spaces are arranged in perfect symmetry. When he is working intensively on a project, he sometimes stays at the Goodenough residency and joins other researchers for meals in the large dining hall of The London House cafeteria.

For several years, Matthew has been diligently working on his translations and submitting articles to support his candidacy for Senior Lecturer. One book of his has been published. If the academic staff, led by Dr. Claire Billington, should vote to promote him, he will gain the academic status important to him. Matthew feels he has much "catching up" to do because he started his academic career rather late. Matthew wants to win the votes of his

colleagues by demonstrating his excellent scholarly abilities to them. Claire, on the other hand, has been pressur-
ing him to lobby for the vote, but he finds the idea of self-
promotion distasteful.

Claire is Professor of Classics and also head of the
department. She is an attractive woman, Matthew acknowledges, who dresses very smartly. In her early forties, with
auburn hair and a trim figure, she seldom wears anything
but Jaeger suits and accessories by Liberty. She carries an
umbrella from James Smith and Company in her expensive
Barrister briefcase. Matthew admires her umbrella with its
unique handle—the head of a bulldog carved in rich, dark
wood. He has noticed her raincoats, also, with their distinctive, Burberry lining. While her wardrobe is not exten-
sive, it is posh, as Londoners like to say.

Matthew thinks Claire is pleasing to look at and her
company is amusing. But he senses she would like a closer
relationship with him, and this makes him uncomfortable
and constantly on his guard.

Well-poised and self-confident, Claire is sometimes per-
ceived as arrogant or aggressive. She had a difficult time
making her way in a field dominated by men, but she is sure
of her approach to scholarship and considers herself avant
garde. Claire is a follower and a passionate advocate of the
postmodern or structuralist school, which emphasizes the
reader's "personal voice." Bringing a subjective interpreta-
tion to the classics, these scholars write about the personal
effect literature has on their lives. For example, Claire
recently published a paper relating the anxieties in her own
life to those of the long-suffering but strong Penelope in
The Odyssey.

Matthew, a traditional scholar and a textural critic,
believes firmly that there is no place in critical theory for

the "personal voice" in classical literature. He considers this type of writing to be "confessional" and not scholarly.

If forced to articulate his values, Matthew would say he pursues the quest for beauty—in words, songs, and art. And, above all, he appreciates adherence to form and tradition. If pushed, he would have to say that he is troubled by what he sees as the decline of standards in the Classics that Claire's "postmodern" approach represents. Matthew has the best of everything, he is sure, and he needs nothing else. He *thinks* he has come to an understanding of who he is.

Because he wants to finish his translations, Matthew has brought his work with him. Manuscript pages are now spread over a long table as he carefully reads and translates. At the other end of the long table are stacks of index cards he uses for his lectures.

Sappho and Aphrodite are now observing Matthew, commenting on how serious he appears to be about his work. "I have never seen a mortal who is more focused," Sappho says. "He must learn about 'all things in moderation.'"

"Yes," Aphrodite comments, "all things in moderation, except for love."

It is 3:52 p.m. and Matthew moves toward the stove to put the kettle on. While the water is heating, he prepares a small tray for his afternoon tea. The water boils, and after pouring it into the pot filled with loose tea, Matthew allows it to steep for three minutes. At 4:00 p.m. he takes a break for tea, a custom he seldom varies, and he relaxes on his balcony, all the while thinking about his projects.

Matthew is determined to finish this translation. Even though it will not be published by the time he is examined for the Senior Lectureship, it will be evidence of additional academic achievement. The new work, along with his articles and books already published, should impress his colleagues, he reasons.

After tea, Matthew arises to return to his translating, but notices the skies have suddenly darkened and the once gentle breezes are now more assertive. The sea has become rougher, and Matthew observes that the winds and the sea change rapidly and unexpectedly in the Greek islands.

It is late Saturday evening when Elena begins to prepare herself. She tingles with anticipation. This will be a Mykonos night.

Carefully selecting what she will wear, combing her hair over and over again, applying and re-applying makeup, and turning and spinning before her full-length mirror, Elena is in a happy state of frenzy.

Just before midnight she leaves her apartment, walking slowly through town to Mykonos Bar. She weaves through the crowds in the narrow, cobblestone streets, experiencing the sensation of walking through a raucous, evening street festival.

Diners are still lingering in the tavernas where they are entertained by skilled local musicians performing folk songs. Many of these men have spent their lives perfecting their artistry and are very proud that they are preserving their cultural traditions through folk songs. Soon, the diners now enjoying the folk songs will pack into the discos and Greek nightclubs where the music is loud and blaring.

Grills are placed outside the tavernas in the evenings, and meats, fish, and vegetables are prepared over hot flames as tourists walk by, tempted by the delicacies. Elena loves Mykonos at night and its nighttime scents. Seared lamb. Expensive perfume. Cigarette smoke. Scented candles. Sweet wine. Marijuana. Roasted eggplant. Marijuana.

Around the next corner, Elena reaches Mykonos Bar. It is spirited. DJ's are playing modern Greek music, and soon live musicians will replace the DJ's and play Rhembetiko and other songs. She remembers reading in Athens that it is only the Greeks and the Spaniards who still listen to their own music consistently, and this makes her feel proud.

Flowers are strewn on the dance floor, and balloons that escaped pinpricks float to the ceiling. There are no broken plates on the floor; the night is still young.

Elena moves about freely, sitting awhile with friends, then dancing, and at times just standing quietly by herself, observing the crowd. She is a favorite dance partner of the regulars who frequent the bar and never refuses a partner, so she dances most of the night, except when the men dance arm-over-arm by themselves.

Elena is energized by the music, the atmosphere, and the magic of Mykonos at night. She plans these nights deliberately and spaces them weeks apart, because for her they are too delicious, like having too much candy. She thinks she could live to dance.

When the night slips into morning, the energy is still high and the dancing is more robust. Musicians and dancers alike pride themselves on their abilities to sustain

PETROS   PRIEST   PAN   IRINI   POSEIDON   SAPPHO   APHRODITE

their energy, and this seems to be a point of pride in the Mykonos Bar. Elena is dancing with a group on the dance floor, but when the tempo of the *tsifte teli* increases, she climbs onto the bar and dances solo, as graceful as a poem. Applause from the crowd and flowers thrown in appreciation of her dancing skills encourage her, and she stays above the crowd, dancing seductively.

As the musicians bring the evening to a close, plates are thrown against the wall, and bottles of champagne are popped and squirted on Elena. Laughing, she dances to the end of the bar where her friends take her by the hands and lift her down.

ᏒᏒᏒ

Matthew rises early that Sunday morning and takes the first bus into town. He enjoys solitary walks in Hora on a Sunday morning when all is peaceful and calm;

he likes to walk by the churches and hear the cantors. Heading for the secluded Alefkandra Quarter, he quickens his pace.

In a cove behind the town, rows of old homes with over-hanging balconies are lapped by the sea, just as they have been for hundreds of years. He sits alone at a closed taverna and listens to the rhythm of the waves and the cantors singing from a nearby church. Called "Little Venice," the Alefkandra Quarter is one of the most romantic spots in Mykonos, and its beauty has been captured by artists and photographers from all over the world.

Matthew decides to stroll to the center of town and makes his way slowly as the churches begin to release their congregations. There are hundreds of churches on the small island, and services begin at different times, some as early as 5:30 a.m. The clubs, on the other hand, remain open all night and close in the early morning hours.

On Sunday mornings, worshippers returning to their homes share the streets with night people who have recently left the clubs and discos. Widows wearing traditional black dresses and head scarves pass young women scantily attired; each group stares in amazement at the other, saving their caustic comments for when they are safely out of earshot. Men and women selling produce from their donkeys stand near young rent boys trying to make one more score before the "night" ends. Music from a nearby club is now playing softly, perhaps in deference to hundreds of church bells tolling all over the island.

Matthew turns into a narrow street and passes an icon maker opening early. His walls are decorated with magnificent works of art in the Byzantine style, each an original. On his easel in the center of his studio is an almost completed icon of St. George and the Dragon. When he begins to paint, he will encourage people to watch as he executes his centuries-old craft; he will also explain some techniques. A few doors down another shop owner is preparing to open. He sells handmade leather handbags and sandals, but has a selection of other leather products—harnesses, vests, gloves, whips—for the gay crowd.

Matthew hears the swishing of skirts as he rounds the corner and comes almost face to face with two tipsy drag queens, one with orange-colored hair who is wearing a long purple gown and another queen with purple hair wearing a billowing orange gown. Walking gingerly on stiletto heels, they flirt with him and giggle as they pass, calling him "honey" and "child."

He has almost reached his favorite coffee shop when he hears the swishing sound again and turns to see two orthodox priests walking behind him, their long black robes draped with jeweled crosses; the robes dust the cobblestones. The men are very old, and their shoulder-length hair and beards are snow white. On their heads, tall *klimafyia* sit like crowns.

The restaurant is not yet open, but Matthew sees a group of young men standing there. As he comes closer, he notices a familiar face in the center of the circle and recognizes the man as a famous fashion designer. He cannot remember his name. The man is surrounded by his acolytes—beautifully attired, handsome young men. They are standing near long tables that have been pushed together; many candles recently extinguished are on the table, and wisps of smoke curl around the squat molds. Wax has dripped onto the white cloth, and the scent of incense, jasmine, and rosemary is in the air.

Matthew has seen the designer here before. He speculates that this must be a favorite spot for him and his boys to watch the crowd, and he guesses (correctly) that they probably start the evening here and then come back in the morning for coffee.

Deciding he will pass on the coffee, Matthew takes a left turn to buy a paper before returning to his apartment. Incense is heavy in the air as he passes another church; he looks in to see candles being extinguished as altar cloths are carefully folded and tucked away until next week's service.

People have gathered at the newsstand to wait for the first boat to arrive from Athens with the morning papers. Matthew sees the boat on the horizon; it will dock shortly. He goes into the bakery for a cheese pie and a coffee and hears local women talking about last night's revelries. News travels fast on Mykonos.

"And she was in the taverna all night!! Dancing on the bar!! It was shameless. All night she was there, dancing on the bar!!"

"Ah, someone had herself a Mykonos night," Matthew says to himself as he prepares to find the bus for the ride back.

SAPPHO   APHRODITE

J ames is strolling on the quay with Dina and with Jim, his friend from America, when a man sitting at the outdoor taverna calls to them. It is Stephanos sitting with his companions, Petros and Nikolaos, and they warmly invite the students to join them.

"How are you enjoying the island?" Petros asks. "Great," the students say.

"Tell us what you will do after the seminar," Stephanos asks. "Have you saved any time for hopping about our islands?"

"Yes," James says, "after the seminar, most of us will have two or three weeks to ourselves."

"We plan to island-hop," Dina explains, "because we hear it is easy to travel by ferry from island to island."

"It is," Stephanos replies, "as long as you plan carefully and concentrate on just one of the island groups. You know, there are six groups plus Crete. We happen to be in the Cyclades."

Jim says, "After our seminar we will take the ferry to Santorini, stay for a few days, and then do what all the tourists do—ride the donkeys to the top of the mountain. Then we will return here and island-hop to Paros and Naxos."

"We have saved visits to Tinos and Andros, with stays overnight on both, for our return trip to Athens," Dina explains and adds, "How does that itinerary sound?"

"Very efficient. You will have a wonderful time," Petros, the oldest seafarer, says. "You cannot help but have a good time in Greece. We have an excellent ferry system. To you it is a means to island-hop. To us it is our link to the outside world."

Stephanos adds, "Do you know in the Cyclades there are twenty-six ferry-linked small islands? You can island-hop until you drop!! Also there are many flights from Athens directly to Rhodes or Crete. Greeks who live in Athens go there or to more remote spots for long weekends."

"A friend of mine said he took Olympic Airlines and flew from Athens to Mykonos in less than an hour," James says.

"The best thing Aristotle Onassis did in his lifetime was to create Olympic Airlines," exclaims Nikolaos, the third Greek. "Now we can travel on short hops to some of the best islands and islanders can fly to Athens on business for the day and return home that night."

"I still prefer the sea," Petros says wistfully. "I will always prefer the sea."

"Do you still work on ferries?" Jim asks.

"No," Stephanos says, "we are fishermen now. We all three are retired and live on Mykonos. We just fish."

"Look," Dina exclaims, pointing to a large bird walking calmly around the tables in the taverna. "A pink bird!!"

"Ah ha," says Petros, "that is my namesake. That is Petros, our most famous citizen."

"He's a pelican," says Jim. "A pink pelican."

"Yes," Nikolaos says. "You'll see a lot of him while you are here, and also his mate, Irini. They are the third generation of pink pelicans to live here. They are cherished, because it was after Petros the First came here in the 1950s that Mykonos began to prosper."

"And the pair of pelicans has been here since?" James asks.

"Except when a storm carries one away!! Once, a storm carried Petros far away to our neighboring island, Tinos, and the people there did not want to return him," Nikolaos explains. "There was almost a major incident."

Petros interjects, "We sent a delegation to Tinos and explained the situation. They were reluctant to give him up, but Petros came back with the delegation!!"

"Petros and Irini are our royalty," Stephanos says, "and every morning you will see the fishermen feeding them generously from their catch."

"But tell us more about your plans. Will you go to the southernmost part of Greece? Will you visit Crete?" Nikolaos asks.

"Yes," Dina affirms, "We'll visit Crete and stay there at least four days."

"Only four days in Crete?" Petros asks.

"That's all the time we allotted," James says. "What can you tell us about Crete?"

"Ah, Μεγαλονησος," Nikolaos says, "Μεγαλονησος."

"The big island!!" Stephanos translates.

"The great island!!" Petros translates.

"Tell us more, please," Jim persists.

It is the most Greek of all the islands, because of its long history and the purity of the Greek blood," Petros says, "and it is the fifth largest island in the whole of the Mediterranean."

"It is the crossroads of three continents," Nikolaos explains.

"I have heard about 'the Cretan Soul,'" James says. "Tell us about that."

"Ah," Nikolaos says, "the Cretan Soul. That is for another time; that is a story that stands alone."

▰▰▰

A fax message arrives at the store where Elena buys her canvasses and other supplies; the clerk hurries to Elena's apartment to give her the message. The message, from the couple in Athens who commissioned her to paint scenes of Mykonos, tells her to paint scenes of Delos instead. "We have changed our decorating scheme and scenes of Mykonos will not do," the message reads. "We want paintings of things that were once sacred and majestic. Scenes that show the magnificence of ancient Greece, particularly sacred Delos." Elena is very surprised by this request because the couple had boasted that people came from all over Greece to see their distinctively modern home, and they wanted art to complement the modern décor. "How strange," Elena thinks.

Aphrodite, walking about blissfully, sprinkling stardust in her path, is almost knocked over by Hermes arriving with great speed and in a highly agitated state. He looks for Sappho, but she is not there. "The thrush of the golden-voice directed me to send a message to Elena," Hermes tells Aphrodite. "And did you?" she asks. "I think so, but it is difficult to explain. All I can tell you, sweet goddess, is that I think I am being replaced by a machine. Be happy that no one will ever be able to say that about you!!"

The next day, Matthew is ready to begin the seminar. On the first day of class, the *Hera* takes him and the six members of his class to the island where he will teach. The boat docks near the Sacred Harbor, the landing place for pilgrims in ancient times. Delos is sun-drenched and barren, with only a few trees and little vegetation. It is bejeweled with the ruins of once glorious temples and mansions.

Small in size, the island is only six kilometers long and 1,500 meters wide, but it is monumental in Greek mythology and history. Delos is not only the geographical center of the Cyclades, but was the religious, cultural, and commercial center of ancient Greece.

Elena, with her watercolors, is also there, near The House of Masks. She is happy to paint scenes of Delos instead of Mykonos. It does not matter to her where she paints, as long as it is on the islands. Almost all of the Grecian islands are perfect for painters because the vistas are very deep; horizons appear to be endless. Elena seeks the perfect place to paint where the light reflects in a certain way off the textured surfaces of the ruins. She chooses a spot where the vegetation is dramatic and carefully surveys the scene from all angles, visualizing the entire composition before touching the stubbled paper with her sable brush. Elena paints at a distance from Matthew and his students, but within sight of them.

Matthew assembles the young scholars at the Ancient Theatre, explaining that he is going to begin with an informal discussion on Delos. "I want you to understand the importance of this sacred site where we are now assembled," he says.

"Oh, honored Tenth Muse," Aphrodite says to Sappho, "I have invited your sister, Clio, to join us to hear this lecture." "Good," Sappho replies, "the Muse of History will help him get it right!! And maybe she can inspire his students as well."

Gathering the students around him, he points to the nearby palm tree: "Here is where Apollo, the god of light, was born to Leto of the lovely hair as she leaned against or held onto a palm tree. Leto gave birth to twins, Apollo and his sister Artemis, goddess of hunting."

"Why was Apollo born here?" Kallirroi asks.

"It was the supreme god, Zeus, who impregnated Leto, one of his many playmates and paramours. Fearing that his wife, the fiery Hera, would find out, Zeus created a safe place for Leto to give birth to Apollo and his twin sister, the goddess Artemis."

"Why was this a safe place?" Kallirroi persists.

"Legend has it that this island suddenly appeared in the waves to provide a sheltered place for Leto, far from the eyes of Hera. Can someone tell me what Delos means?" Matthew asks.

"Visible," James offers.

"That which appeared," ventures Dina.

"Yes, both are correct."

"When was the island first inhabited?" another student, Brandon, asks.

Shuffling his small index cards on which he keeps factual information, Matthew says, "Most likely it was inhabited in 3,000 B.C. We know that at the end of the fourth century it developed into a major commercial center, competing with Rhodes. By Roman times, Delos had roughly 25,000 inhabitants, more or less. Archaeologists uncovered evidence of Ionians living here in the 7th Century B.C., followed through the centuries by Athenians, Delians, Egyptians, Syrians, and Romans."

"It must have been a jewel in the Aegean sea," Brandon comments.

"It was," Matthew responds, "and it probably served as a 'summer home' for the wealthy who lived on the islands that formed a circle around Delos. It was magnificent and majestic."

"Did Egypt's Queen Cleopatra ever live here?" Kallirroi asks.

"That story is not true," Matthew says. "I don't know how it originated. There is no evidence she ever lived here."

After just a few more facts about the island, Matthew explains, they will move on to the poetry.

"Delos' rule over the sea was established around 478 B.C. when a Delian Confederacy was formed to bring neighboring islands under its influence, thus establishing

Delos' supremacy," he begins. "During this time, lavish festivals were held every five years to honor the gods. Large barges brought animals from neighboring islands here for slaughter as sacrifices, and the most nubile Delian maidens were chosen to dance and sing hymns in honor of the gods."

He explains that the "sacred" island was once a burial ground for Delians. "Sometime around 426 B.C., to secure the favor of Apollo and, incidentally, to gain control of the shrine's treasures, the bones of those who died here were removed to a nearby island where a new burial ground was created. Also, from that point forward, women who were about to give birth on the sacred land were taken to that same nearby island.

"In effect, no one could be born on Delos, nor could the dead remain here.

"Today, the government forbids anyone to live here or stay overnight," he tells the enthralled students. "Can anyone tell us the history of this island's fall?"

Jim responds: "It was a sudden, brutal fall in 88 B.C. during the Mithridatic War. All inhabitants—estimates range from 20,000 to 30,000—were slaughtered, and the mansions and temples desecrated and demolished."

"Correct. What happened next?" Matthew prompts.

James continues the story. "Delos was burned by a victorious army of barbarians," he says.

"And...," Matthew prompts again.

"Years later, pirates came regularly to the island to pick over the remains. It was not until late in the nineteenth century that archaeologists began excavations that revealed the glory of Delos and encouraged the Greek government to establish strict rules for this sacred site."

Clio dances with delight as Sappho and Aphrodite congratulate her.

"Well done," Matthew says, "exceptionally well done. In fact, very inspired.

"To bring you up to the present, let me add that the French School of Archeology began excavations in 1872, and in 1904 what is known as 'the great excavation' took place. This is when many public buildings and private houses were uncovered and some were partly reconstructed. Work is still in progress."

Matthew pauses, placing a rubber band around his index cards. "Let's break for lunch. For those of you who did not bring your lunches, you can get something in the snack bar in the museum over there. After the break, I'll begin the lecture on Sappho. Does anyone have any questions at this time?"

Dina asks, "Was Sappho a lesbian?"

"Yes," Matthew responds immediately and without qualification.

The students are surprised, and Dina asks, "How does one know?"

"Because she was born on the island of Lesbos and was, therefore, a Lesbian," Matthew replies with twinkling eyes, but straight face.

Laughing, the students make no further attempt at eliciting information from Matthew on Sappho's sexual preference.

᠎᠎᠎

*S*appho, Clio, and Aphrodite observe this scene with great interest, wondering how Matthew will present Sappho's poetry. "How strange that these young people do not know I am a Lesbian," Sappho whispers to Aphrodite. "By now, everyone should know I was born on Lesbos."

"Perhaps they have little interest in geography, golden sister," Clio says with a worried frown.

"Yes," agrees Aphrodite, who is noted as a wise goddess. She has had much more experience with mortals than Sappho. Aphrodite whispers to Clio that she is a bit concerned about how information on Sappho's life will be presented and how Sappho will react. Clio nods in understanding and appears to be musing on what can be done.

The students return after lunch, eager to hear Matthew's opening lecture.

"Listen, Sappho," Aphrodite says, "Clio and I think this will be boring to you. He is going to tell all about your wonderful accomplishments and your long, lovely life, and then he will talk about your lyrics. Why don't you find the other Muses and bring them here so we can listen to your lyrics together?"

"That is a wonderful idea," Sappho says. "It will be boring to listen to this part of the lecture when I know what he is going to say. Clio, wait here. I will gather our eight sisters." Sappho races through the clouds to a nearby mountain.

The students sit in a semicircle and take notes as Matthew begins his lecture:

"Many scholars agree that Sappho is the greatest lyric poet of antiquity. Facts about her life are few, but the legend of how she lived and died make her one of the most fascinating women in literature. What is undisputed is that she was born on the island of Lesbos at either Mytilene or Eresus, lived between 630 and 570 B.C., and wrote nine books of poetry that were collected by others after her death. This collection is lost. And then the legend takes over.

"Most historians believe she was married to a rich man, 'Cercylas of Andros,' and had a daughter named 'Clais' or 'Cleis,' whom she adored and honored in poems. A few others find no evidence that she was married and believe the 'Cleis' to whom she wrote poems meant simply 'child,' but not necessarily her child. It is believed that Sappho was well-educated and refined in the arts and lived for a time in Sicily. When she returned to Lesbos, she lived 'in the society of young girls.'

"Any questions so far?"

"What does 'living in the society of young girls' mean?" Jim asks.

"This is the source of her legend. It has never been defined and we will never know exactly what 'living in the society of young girls' means or meant. Was she their teacher? Was she their lover? Was she simply writing witty poetry? We will never know."

"How did Sappho see herself?" Kallirroi questions.

"Sappho saw herself as 'The Tenth Muse' and wrote in one poem that 'the violet weaving muses' had blessed her. In another poem she predicted her place in history. She wrote:

> YES
> The golden Muses
> have given me true fame,
> and once I am dead
> my words shall live forever!!

"Sappho's poetry is extraordinary. She wrote tender, erotic poetry about love for women and love between women. To a woman she admired she wrote:

> I do not think any girl
> who will look upon
> the sun's light
> will possess your skill.

"To another she said simply:

"'You burn me.'

"Of all the poems Sappho wrote, just a few survive, but what we have are quite marvelous. In a study devoted to female poets, Sappho's name appears above a blank page as a dramatic way to inform the reader that, tragically, much of her work is lost. A small collection of 'complete' poems and fragments remains, but her nine books of poetry, carefully collected by scholars in Alexandria many years after her death, have gone missing.

"The legend, however, lives. Some critics believe Sappho ran a type of finishing school for young women, teaching the art of living through music and poetry; others speculate that she was highly skilled in the art of lovemaking."

Aphrodite is aghast, pacing to and fro and trying to keep her composure. Clio is taking notes.

"What was that noise?" Matthew asks. "Did you hear a shriek?"

"Didn't hear a thing," Dina says. "Tell us, how did Sappho die?"

"We don't know, but the legend concerning her death is drama of the highest form. Through the centuries, many people have believed that Sappho committed suicide by leaping into the sea from a high rock on the island of Leucadia. According to one version of this story, she was in despair over love for Phaon, a ferryman. But he never existed. He is a purely mythological figure. In the myth, Phaon ferries the goddess Aphrodite, disguised as an old woman, across a river. When the boatman does not ask her for payment, the charmed Aphrodite transforms him into a beautiful youth who is then adored by all the women of Lesbos."

Matthew stops. "There's that noise again."

Aphrodite quickly places her hand over her mouth, resumes her pacing, and looks anxiously toward Mt. Helicon. Clio is mumbling words Aphrodite cannot understand, but they sound like "revisionist and deconstructionism."

"Does anyone know the source of these stories?" James asks.

"Some scholars attribute the story of Sappho's suicide to the humor of the Attic comic dramatists and give it no credence. They say it would have appealed to these comedians to invent a story of Sappho's passion for a man, and for a man who never existed!

"We will now move onto the recitations," Matthew concludes.

ϿϿϿ

A*t this moment, Sappho returns from Mt. Helicon, accompanied by the eight other muses. They are splendidly attired with violet wreaths adorning their heads and long robes flowing from their shoulders. The muses are daughters of Zeus and Memory, and each has her own specialty and special powers.*

Seated from left to right are Urania, Muse of astronomy; Melpomene, of tragedy; Thalia, of comedy; Terpsichore, of dance; Calliope, of epic poetry; Erato, of love poetry; Polyhymnia, of songs to the gods; and Euterpe, of lyric poetry. Clio joins her sisters.

"Sappho," Aphrodite says, "I offer you pride of place. You sit on the right with the other muses, and I will sit here. Let us enjoy your songs."

"How can he teach my lyrics without a lyre?" Sappho asks. "I do not see a lyre. How strange these mortals are."

The students prepare to read translations they completed last night as homework assignments, and Elena moves about trying other perspectives for her paintings. As she moves toward the class, the students have agreed upon the translated lines they think best represents the meaning of the poem. Matthew asks James to read the results of their efforts. He reads:

> Some say
> a company of horsemen,
> others a legion of foot soldiers,
> and others a fleet of ships
> is the most beautiful to behold
> on this black earth;
> I say
> the most beautiful
> is whomever
> one loves.

"Well done," Matthew says. "This is one of Sappho's most memorable poems and is quoted often. It is famous for the line 'The most beautiful is whomever one loves.' Remember that line; we will come back to it.

"Let's try another. The lovely poem we will examine now describes the agony of women at the funeral of a young woman they once had loved, but who left them for marriage. I would like each of you to read me a few lines." When they finish, Karen volunteers to read the entire translation:

> This is the dust of Timas
> who unmarried was led
> into Persephone's dark bedroom
> And many maidens from her home

mourned for her with tears.
And knowing she would not return,
took sharpened shears
And cut the curls of their soft hair.

The muses are impressed and gather round Sappho. "Aphrodite, Aphrodite," Sappho says, "how lovely!! I said those words so long ago. Who is this man who now honors me so by teaching my songs?"

Aphrodite says, " We must reward him, golden thrush."

"Yes, we must," agrees Sappho, as she sends a brilliant flash of light through the clear blue sky. It crackles like a thunderbolt and is gone within seconds.

Matthew's and Elena's eyes lock during the flash of light, and neither can look away until the brilliance subsides. Slowly, Elena walks away, but looks backward to see Matthew peering over his glasses at her. Then he slowly turns his attention once again to his class.

"We will meet here again tomorrow," he tells the students. "I feel very inspired. Before we leave, let us look at the first poem translated again."

With difficulty, Matthew tries to concentrate.

"We have all heard the popular phrase, 'Beauty is in the eye of the beholder,'" he says. "Do you have an idea now of the origin of that expression?"

"Yes," Brandon responds, "it is from Sappho's line, 'It is whatsoever a person loves.'"

"Can that be translated still another way?" Matthew asks, struggling to concentrate.

"Yes," Brandon answers, "I say the most beautiful sight is the beloved."

Matthew does not respond. He is distracted, turning his back to the class, watching Elena as she walks away. Elena has turned once more to look at him.

"Bravo! Bravo!" shout the muses, as all applaud the recitations. Sappho is delighted and wonders why Aphrodite breathes a sigh of relief.

Near the Hotel Nissaki is the Hotel Akrogiali; here, Yannis, who wants to be Elena's suitor, is employed as a waiter. Yannis is a very handsome young Greek with dark, deep-set eyes, high cheekbones, and thick, black hair. His black trousers and white shirt are always perfectly pressed and he takes pride in his neat appearance. He has a quick, nervous laugh which one hears before Yannis speaks. People always smile when first meeting him, and women are drawn to him. He is an ambitious young man who works eighteen hours a day as a waiter from April to October during the tourist season. At the end of the season, he returns to his home in Castoria, Northern Greece, the center of a major fur industry. In Castoria, he labors many hours a day processing fox and mink pelts.

Yannis is one of an army of young Macedonians from Northern Greece who come south year after year to the resort islands to serve the tourists. He has been doing this for ten years with a short break for military service, but he longs to earn enough money in a few years to live a simple life in Northern Greece. And his dream is to marry Elena and take her home with him.

Numerous cruise ships, large and small, dock at Mykonos harbor; the tourists pour into the beachfront hotels, especially the Akrogiali, for lunch. On a typical day, Yannis serves eight to ten lunch tables at once, whirling between the tables and speaking to the guests in their native tongues—French, Italian, German, or English. He has learned enough of each language to master basic conversation, and he delights in serving appreciative guests. His engaging, amicable personality and his "fluency" in other languages result in his being assigned more tables than the other waiters who speak only Greek and limited English. So Yannis works harder and earns more money than everyone else.

"*L'homard et spaghetti est mieux!!*" Yannis says in French to his table of French tourists. "*C'est mieux!!*" (The lobster and spaghetti is the best!! It is the best!!)

This entree also happens to be the most expensive on the menu. Since Yannis receives a percentage of everything he sells, he is always pleased when his guests order the lobster. The young man moves quickly and gracefully to the kitchen to place the order and returns with food for another table. Holding a huge tray of hot, steaming food high above his head, he seems to swing between the tables, managing the heavy tray with perfect balance. It is overflowing with platters of grilled lobsters sprinkled generously with brown butter and a few herbs. In the bright red lobster shells are mounds of spaghetti in a marinara sauce that Yannis proclaims is "fresh, fresh—specially made with fresh tomatoes, fresh olive oil, and fresh basil—everything is fresh—it is the best!" As he returns to the kitchen, he is stopped by a woman at a table where the diners have just completed their meal.

The American woman asks, then begs him for the recipe for the lobster and spaghetti. "Please no," says Yannis, "I cannot, Madame, because it is a secret."

Shortly thereafter, a Greek woman dressed in very expensive clothing and wearing spectacular gold earrings, bracelets, and a large necklace makes the same request, which Yannis denies. Each day he is asked for this recipe several times, and each time he has to keep the secret. He dashes to the kitchen, returning with another steaming tray. And so the day goes. The work seems to be without end. Home at 2 a.m., a few hours sleep, and back to the hotel by 7 a.m.

Throughout the long days and nights, Yannis serves tourists who come from all over the world. Some have obviously saved their money for this vacation and spend carefully (Yannis can tell by the way they order), but most are extremely wealthy and spend freely. Because he works so hard to support himself, the young man cannot imagine spending money as freely as the guests he serves. And he himself could never sit idly for hours on the beach chairs. "How can they enjoy life sitting still?" he thinks, hurrying to take a tray of drinks to a group of them.

Yannis manages to take a few hours at slow times to search for Elena at Mykonos Bar, located in the part of Mykonos known as "Little Venice." Natives of Mykonos meet here, along with Greek tourists who know they will find the best Greek dancing here. On the rare occasions

when he happens to see Elena, he pleads his case passionately. He tells her he is saving all his money to live the
good life in in Northern Greece. "We can have a good
future here," he tells her, "and you will have the best of
everything. Every night, Elena, lobster and spaghetti!!" But
Elena has told him many times that she will never leave
Mykonos, even though some of her memories here are
painful.

On the second day of the seminar, Matthew goes to Delos hours before class is scheduled to begin; he needs to decide where he will conduct his future lectures. Before disembarking the *Hera*, he sees Elena on board. Carrying her portfolio and art materials, she mingles with the boat's crew and the tour guide. Matthew approaches her once they are off the boat.

"Καλημερα," he begins in Greek, as he runs his fingers through his thick, wind-blown hair. Then, believing that it should be Elena's choice to continue the conversation in the language of her choice, he says in English, "I saw you on the *Penelope* when we arrived here, and yesterday I noticed you painting near my class."

"Yes," she says, choosing to converse in English, "I noticed you as well."

"I'm walking toward the Sacred Lake," Matthew says. "Are you going that way?"

"Yes I am," Elena answers and then finds herself explaining, "I have to complete some sketches. In fact, I received a fax last night from the couple who have commissioned me telling me they want scenes of the lions guarding the Sacred Lake, and also some paintings of the mosaics."

"I'm teaching a seminar here, in fact near the Sacred Lake, and I plan to give my last lecture at the Archaeological Museum," Matthew explains.

"It would be very interesting to teach some sessions at the House of Dionysus or the House of the Masks," Elena suggests.

"Yes, I plan to teach there so the students can see the mosaics. Is that why you suggest those sites?" Matthew asks.

"Exactly. Those once-magnificent mosaic floors have survived through the centuries," she declares.

"The mosaics are precious," Matthew agrees, then asks, "Where did you say you will be painting today?"

"Near the museum."

"That is where I will be teaching," Matthew says. "Do you mind?"

"Not at all," Elena laughs. "Do you mind if I listen to your class?"

"You are welcome to join the class," Matthew says. "If you like, I will invite you to recite some poetry."

"No thanks," says Elena, "I prefer just to listen. I find it very peaceful here, where there is less idle talk or even heated debates as in Mykonos. It makes me tired!"

"What is being debated in Mykonos?"

"A new marina, a new airport!! Expansion, expansion!! I need to think about more pleasant subjects."

"That is all the more reason you should join my class. We will be translating lovely poetry, which should take your mind off such things. Perhaps you can help us with the translations? You could teach my students how Greek should be spoken."

"Thank you—joining your class sounds like a good idea, but if you don't mind, I will just listen."

"You are most welcome," Matthew says. "I'll see you in about an hour near the museum."

"I look forward to it," Elena says. "I know you are teaching poetry. For some strange reason last night I searched for my book of Sappho's poems, which I haven't looked at since high school. Are you teaching only her poetry?"

"Yes," Matthew says, looking directly at Elena over the top of his glasses, "only the poetry of Sappho. See you soon."

ᄅᄅᄅ

When the afternoon session begins, Elena paints nearby, deliberately remaining within earshot of the class. Her strokes are deft and bold. When one is using watercolors, there is little room for error. But she is continually distracted by her growing interest in the class discussion.

The students are reading, and Matthew is explicating some of the poems. They are discussing fragments.

"Straightaway, at my bedside stands golden-sandaled Dawn," James translates from the Greek.

"Straightaway?" Matthew asks. "Is that an exact translation? Would the ancients have said 'straightaway?'"

"Suppose not. Shall I try again?"

"Please do."

"Suddenly, at my bedside stands golden-sandaled Dawn."

"Very good."

"Is this a poem or a fragment?" Kallirroi asks.

Matthew replies, "Does it express a complete thought?"

"Yes."

"The critics may differ," Matthew says, "but to my mind, since it is a complete thought, it is a poem."

The image of a golden-sandaled dawn brings a smile to Elena's face. She stays close by, but makes no overture. Matthew's memory of her from the *Penelope* is vivid, but he observes that her long tresses are now held on the top of her head by a barrette.

Matthew turns his attention again to the class.

"Let's start with a definition of a poem. Can anyone give us one?" he asks. "One definition I like is by Wordsworth; does anyone remember it?"

Kallirroi answers. "Yes, Wordsworth said a poem is 'a spontaneous overflow of powerful feelings.'"

"Yes, excellent," Matthew says, and then asks for an example of one of Sappho's poems which meets this definition.

After some false starts, the students agree that one poem they have studied is an outstanding expression of powerful feelings. The poem begins with these lines:

Φαινεται μοι κηνος ισος θεοισιν
εμμεν ωνηρ οττις εναντιος τοι
ισδανει και πλασιον αδυ φωνει–σας υπακουει

"Who will take the first line?" Matthew asks.

Dina volunteers: "'He seems as a god to me.' Or 'He appears to be a god to me.'"

"Good, very good, and the next line?"

James, the British student, raises his hand. Smiling broadly, he translates:

> "He seems as a god to me,
> that bloke who sits beside you."

Stopping, he waits for Matthew's reaction.

"That bloke!!" Matthew laughs along with the class.

"I don't think you can get 'bloke' from the Greek text. Not from the words used by Sappho. Want to try again?"

"Well, I like bloke, but how about 'that man who sits beside you?'"

"That's better. Who is the next volunteer?"

Taking turns, they haltingly recite, translate, and explicate lines from one of Sappho's most famous poems. Matthew gently corrects the translations and encourages the entire class to participate.

It is a long poem, requiring patience and careful attention. When they are finished, Matthew recites the poem, in Greek and then in English:

> That man appears to be a god to me,
> who sits opposite you,
> and savors your sweet voice
> and lovely laughter.
> Surely, my heart trembles in my breast,
> for when I look upon you for a moment,
> I lose my voice, cannot speak.
> My tongue is silent.
> Suddenly a fire races under my skin,
> I see nothing, my ears hum,
> And I begin to sweat and tremble.
> I am greener than grass
> and a breath away from dying.
>
> .

Matthew pauses after this recitation and asks the students for comments. They are reluctant to begin, so Matthew prods.

"In the first line, to whom does Sappho compare the man sitting next to the one who is beloved?"

"She compares him to the gods," Jim answers.

"Correct—he is as a god. And how does Sappho describe what happens to her as she watches?"

"She says she trembles, cannot speak, cannot hear," Kallirroi ventures.

"True, now take that a step further and examine exactly how she is describing her emotions."

"She describes what is happening through the senses," James answers. "First she trembles, then she cannot speak, see, nor hear."

"Very good, very good," Matthew compliments the student. "What else is going on in this poem?"

"There are extreme emotions," Brandon says. "The poet both freezes—she says it is not possible to speak—and she burns—she says a subtle fire has stolen her flesh."

"Excellent, excellent. Now how can we sum up this lovely poem? What do you think Sappho was trying to do?"

"I think she was being very witty," Dina says.

"Yes," Jim says, "witty and whimsical."

"What is she trying to describe?" Matthew asks. "What is happening to Sappho and what is she describing?"

Kallirroi says, "She is describing, in her witty, inimitable way, a person who has fallen in love."

"Bravo, bravo," Matthew declares.

"Now tell me, class," Matthew continues, "how intense is this love?"

"It is so intense that she feels she is about to die," comes the reply.

"Tell me again," Matthew asks, "what is the definition of a poem?"

"A spontaneous overflow of powerful feelings," James says confidently.

"Would you agree, then," Matthew concludes, "that this poem meets that description?"

The students, who are very animated, agree:

"Yes, yes."

"Most certainly."

"Very powerful."

Elena, who has heard the translation and discussion, is amused and impressed. As she has seen how Matthew guided the students through this extraordinary poem, her admiration has grown. She smiles at Matthew, communicating her approval. Matthew, who is flushed with the success of his pedagogy, returns Elena's smile.

Sappho, singing sweetly on heaven's highest cloud, is watching over the pair. Aphrodite and the Muses are by her side. "Did I not tell you, Golden Sister," Sappho asks gleefully, "that my words will live forever?"

"Your words make them burn, Sappho," Aphrodite says, "but we must not act with haste because the messenger, Hermes, has not yet located the god Poseidon, lord of the sea. We shall soon need his help."

"Yes, my golden-throned sister, we shall," Sappho sings, "we certainly shall."

Early that evening, James and Jim go to Matthew's flat to tell him about an island-hop they have been planning.

"Dr. Wyttman," James, the British student says, "Jim and I plan to take advantage of our time in Greece by seeing some important historical sites, and we wanted to ask your opinion."

"Of course, James, what would you like to see? And please call me Matthew."

"Thank you, Dr.—I mean, Matthew. We are interested in visiting the tomb of Homer on the Island of Ios. Do you think that would be a worthwhile trip?"

"You understand, it is just legend that says Homer is buried there. Some people say there is a prehistoric tomb there and others say there is not. Of course it would be an important, historical place to visit, and I am impressed by your interest. Imagine telling your classmates when you return to the U.K. that you were on the island where Homer last walked!!"

"Yes," says Jim, the American student, "and I can tell my friends the same story as well."

"Well, off you go for the weekend, then," Matthew says. "The ferry service to Ios is quite regular. Remember, I'm responsible for your safety, so be sure to let me know if your return journey is delayed for any reason. Keep my phone number with you. It's the norm for sea conditions to change quickly here, and choppy seas could delay you."

ᄅᄅᄅ

The Island of Ios lies between Naxos and Santorini in the southeastern Cyclades and is one of the most popular destinations for tourists from throughout Europe. Not all tourists, however, come to this island to visit the alleged resting place of Homer.

James and Jim arrive in the early morning and head for the ruins at Plakoto, said to be the site of the tomb. An excavation is in progress; the young men inquire about the dig.

"We have permission to open this tomb and see if it contains the old man's remains," an archaeologist explains. "We're going to do DNA tests and all of that. Don't come too close now—we've gone pretty deep."

"Can you imagine?" James exclaims. "This is pure luck that we are here at this very time when they may actually open the tomb of Homer!! Unbelievable!!"

"Unbelievable," agrees Jim.

As directed, they move to the side and watch the dig from there.

"I discuss Homer quite a bit in my essay," Jim says, taking the paper from his backpack. "I brought it with me to show you and make revisions."

"Great, I want to read it. But how did you tie it in with Sappho?"

"I was struck by the difference in the way Sappho writes in comparison to Homer. I examined Sappho's imagery; I think she chose some of these images because, as a woman, this is how she saw the world," James explains. "She's certainly not a female Homer. A man sees things differently."

There is a great rumbling in the clouds. On the highest cloud, Sappho jumps from her throne, calling to Aphrodite. "A female Homer, a female Homer!! Did you hear that, Aphrodite? What does he mean by 'A female Homer'?"

Aphrodite attempts to calm her, but Sappho is indeed in a rage. "How dare these silly boys study my poetry and not know that I am a lyric poet? Homer is our great epic poet!! Don't they know the difference between a lyric poem and an epic poem? We should have asked my sisters Calliope, the Muse of epic poetry, and Euterpe, the Muse of lyric poetry, to watch over the boys. They will pay for their silliness!!"

Unaware of the furor they've caused, the young men decide to move closer to the excavation. The archaeologists are preoccupied. The huge hole they have dug is so deep that all they can see is blackness. Jim, holding his essay in his hand, peers deeper into the hole. A sudden gust of wind whirls by, and the paper is torn from him, landing in the pit of the cave!!

"My essay, my essay!" Jim shouts. "Where did that wind come from?"

"Wow, that was strong," says James. "Your paper is gone. Do you have another copy?"

"No. This entrance they've dug can't be that deep. Maybe it just looks a lot blacker than it is. Let's try to crawl down."

"You go first."

"It's your paper, you go first."

"Well, let's try it together," James says, but as he walks around the excavation, the archaeologist sees them and shouts: "Get away from the excavation, it's very deep. Move away!!"

"That's it. You can forget about your paper."

"No, no, oh what will I do now?"

"Let's walk further along the island and figure something out."

Sappho has just begun her mischief. She is not satisfied to use just the powers of the gods of the winds. For her next scheme she needs still another god. "Quickly, Aphrodite," Sappho orders, "summon Dionysus and tell him to bring powerful potions dipped in wine and wrapped in flowers."

The hapless young men are now strolling on Mylopotas Beach, which a young person on the ferry described as "one of the best beaches in the Aegean." They seek a camping site and finally select "Far Out Camping," where they set up their tent.

"Hey, dude," an American camper calls lazily, "mellow out and have a piece of fruit."

"Mellow out with fruit?" Jim asks.

"This fruit will do it!!"

"Thanks," James says, "we didn't have anything to eat on the ferry."

"Here's some fruit for you, too," the camper offers, giving another piece to Jim. "Mellow out."

"This has such a sweet taste, like honey," James declares with delight.

"And it is as soft as a flower," Jim adds.

Eating the fruit with gusto, James and Jim join the campers, who offer more fruit and wine.

"See that pavilion back there?" the camper asks, pointing to a bar area that is almost deserted. "The rock band starts at three o'clock, and by three-fifteen everyone is dancing on the tables."

"I thought this island was noted for being the site of the tomb of Homer," Jim says.

"Who is this Homer dude and what's this about a tomb, man?" the camper asks. "Ios is *the* party island of Greece."

"We came to…" James begins, but stops when Jim interrupts by asking, "Three o'clock did you say?"

Well past six o'clock, James and Jim are still dancing on the tables to the pounding rock music of the group, "Acropolis Now!!" By eight o'clock, they are stretched out on their backpacks. The music is still blaring.

"I'm mellowed out," says James.

"Have another piece of fruit," offers Jim.

Gleefully, Sappho watches from above. Aphrodite, who does not approve of Sappho's mischief, has moved to another cloud and has summoned the god Apollo. He, the god of light and reason, plays sweet music on his golden lyre for Aphrodite, who is now using all her powers of love on him. With sweet laughter, she flirts and praises his good looks and his musicianship. "No one in all of Olympus is as fair as you or plays music as sweet as yours," she tells him, tossing her flowing hair over her purple mantle. Delighted, Apollo composes a new song especially for her.

"Apollo," Aphrodite says, "I need a favor."

"Certainly, my goddess."

"An Olympian favor."

"Anything, my goddess, anything," Apollo promises.

"You must rescue two mortals who unwittingly offended Sappho, our great muse," Aphrodite explains. *"I will not tell you their offense for fear that Sappho will hear those words spoken again, but I do believe they have learned a lesson. Now they must be rescued from those drinking wine and eating powerful potions. They must be set free so they can redeem themselves."*

"Of course, my lovely daughter of Zeus, you beguile me with your wisdom. As long as light and reason will enter their souls, we must set them free. It is as good as done," Apollo declares, vanishing.

James and Jim are mellow, alternately listening to the music and dozing for brief periods. Awake now, they seek the campers who gave them refreshments, but don't find them.

"They've gone, man, left with the others," a very handsome young man with blonde curly hair says.

"Where'd they go? Is there a better party somewhere else?"

"No, they and the others went to visit the tomb of Homer," the perfectly formed, gorgeous man explains.

All of a sudden James and Jim notice that the rock band is now playing classical music!!

A vendor is walking along the beach selling lemonade.

"My head is suddenly clear," Jim says, "and I have another idea for my essay."

"Great," James says. "What will you write about?"

"I am going to examine Sappho's lovely imagery and her invention of a distinctive meter which became known as the sapphic meter."

"You are not going to compare her with Home...?"

"Please, please don't say that. Hurry, let's get the next ferry and I will write my homage to Sappho's timeless lyrics on the way back to Mykonos."

ᄅᄅᄅ

B ack in Mykonos, as Matthew returns to his flat the manager calls to him, saying there is a telephone message. He hands him a slip of paper.

"I took the message as best I could, but I couldn't understand everything the boys were saying."

"Really??" Matthew responds.

"This message says they are on their way back to Mykonos, but Jim needs time to write another paper. It says the paper he wrote fell down Homer's tomb."

"Let's see if I have this right," Matthew says and then slowly reads, "The paper fell down Homer's tomb."

"Yes," the manager says.

Matthew, still incredulous, asks, "And the boys are coming home, but because the paper fell down the tomb, James needs time to write another paper with a new topic, about the glorious verses of the poet Sappho?"

"No, Jim needs time to write another paper."

"Well, I have heard many excuses for a late paper, but this is the most cryptic," Matthew says.

"Perhaps they simply had a misadventure," the manager speculates.

"Yes, indeed, they could have had a bad trip," Matthew says gravely.

It is mid-morning, and Yannis parks his moped and hurries
into the Hotel Akrogiali. He goes straight to the bar, picks
up a pack of matches, moves to the far corner of the patio,
and hungrily lights a cigarette.

"Ah," Yannis says, "ah, that's good.

"Γεια σου, Γιαννη, γεια σου," (Hi there, Yannis, hi
there.) Costas, the older waiter says, acknowledging his
presence.

"You act as though you haven't had a cigarette for half a
day," Costas says.

"As the Americans say, 'you've got that right.' It's been
that long."

"Why, no money to buy them? With all the tips you
make?"

"No, no matches."

"Why didn't you ask those tourists staying down the hall from your room?"

"Costas," Yannis says evenly, "you should know by now that I do not ask anybody for anything."

"But a simple match? You wouldn't ask?"

"Right. I just decided I would go to sleep. Then, when I woke up I came right here and now I have my cigarette. What do Americans say? 'No big deal.'"

"Whatever you say. No big deal," Costas says, shaking his head in disbelief.

The dining room manager comes onto the patio and calls to the waiters.

"Yannis, Costas, new groups of tourists have arrived and are coming here for a late breakfast. Just checked in. They have the usual questions, Yannis, so you talk to them and give them the answers. Americans and Germans. And French newlyweds!!"

The newlyweds are seated first and after Costas takes their order, Yannis approaches and greets them.

"*Bonjour, bonjour,*" Yannis says, "*Bien-venu à Mykonos.*"

"*Bonjour, bonjour,*" the young couple say, radiating happiness. The man begins a conversation with Yannis about Mykonos and asks if he could recommend a special restaurant.

"Ah, but we have the best food here, of course," Yannis says. "Our lobster and spaghetti dinner is the best on the island."

"I am sure of it," the man says, "but let's say you were going out some night for a change of scenery; where would you go to dine?"

"I rarely get a night off," Yannis says, "but on the night that is mine, I always go to Katrina's. Katrina has the best seafood on the island. And very romantic. Yes, I always go to Katrina's."

Yannis excuses himself and hurries to a table at the other end of the patio where a group of young men and women has settled in.

"Waiter," a young woman says in English, "we just got here and we're looking for the 'in spot' on Mykonos. Where does everyone go to dance?"

"You may like The Veranda Club," Yannis offers.

"Is it really special? Is that where people hang out?"

"Yes," Yannis says, "it is where I go on my night off. It is where I hang out."

"Well thank you," a young man at the table says. "If you go there, that must be the place to go!!"

Yannis moves toward another table of new arrivals.

"Entschuldigen Sie bitte, der Manager sagte, Sie konnten mir helfen?" (Excuse me, the manager said you could help us?)

"Ja gerne. Wie kann ich Ihnen behilflich sein?" Yannis replies to the elderly woman. (Yes, gladly, how can I be of help?)

The woman asks where she and her friends can find classical music. She wants to know if there are concerts anywhere on Mykonos and explains they will be here for two weeks.

"Wednesday nights in the Town Hall," Yannis says enthusiastically in her language. "Retired classical musicians get together every Wednesday night for—how do you say?—a string quartette."

The woman is most pleased and says, "Oh, how wonderful, are they good?"

"Yes, madam, very good. If my night off comes on a Wednesday, that is where I go to hear the musicians."

"Danke viel mals, junger mann." (Thank you very much, young man.)

Halfway to the kitchen, Yannis is stopped again by a plea from Costas.

"Yannis, come here please, these gentlemen from America have some questions."

"Ah, gentlemen," Yannis says in English, "may I take your orders first?"

"Yes, please, I'll have coffee and a pastry."

"That sounds good, I'll have the same," the second man says, as the man to his left says, "Make it three."

"And you, Sir?" asks Yannis of the fourth man.

"I'll have milk and cookies," he giggles.

"You always have to be different," chides his companion and everyone laughs happily as Yannis heads for the kitchen to place the order.

When Yannis returns, the men ask him about gay bars on Mykonos, and the questions come spilling out.

"Where is the action?" the man asks.

"Where can we find the drag queens?"

"Where do you go on your night off?"

"I never have a night off," Yannis says, eyes straight ahead, as he carefully gives each man his order.

On a week night in the early evening, the parade to the Town Hall begins slowly. The elderly are first to arrive, and many come walking in front of their donkeys. The baskets on the donkeys, which in the morning overflowed with fresh fruit and vegetables, are now empty, but will be filled again the next day. There is no practical reason for the donkeys to be with the old men and women this particular night, but it is the habit of the elderly to keep their beasts with them when they walk around the island. What is unusual is the destination—the Town Hall.

Next the tourists see bearded Greek Orthodox priests, with large silver crosses draped over their long black robes and their silver heads of hair crowned by the tall hat that is called a *klimafi*. They are following the elderly and talking with them and each other in a very animated fashion.

Couples arrive, some with and others without children. Groups of family members and friends also make their way to the Town Hall, and by 6:30 p.m. all the seats are taken and a large crowd stands at the back of the room.

Elena knows it is important to attend this meeting, but, unaccountably, she had a strong desire to stay at home and read Sappho. Her thoughts are on Matthew.

Reluctantly, she decides to join her friends who are now assembled near the front of the room to the left. Since hearing the latest unsettling news, Elena's friends have gathered 900 signatures in just two days. They worked very efficiently to accomplish this task and are now determined to present the petition. On the opposite side of the room are Elena's parents and members of her extended family. They nod to her in recognition, and she returns their greeting.

It is unusual to have a meeting of this type on Mykonos. Old-timers—such as the retired seafarers, Stephanos, Nikolaos, and Petros—remember a similar meeting fifteen years ago. They were present during that first meeting when everyone was called together to discuss developing the beachfront, and the luxury hotels that now serve the tourists.

Elena's father, Tassos, is restless and moves to the back of the hall to join his good friend, Nikolaos. They talk quietly. He reminds Mr. Angelides that he has not been fishing with the three of them for quite a while and Tassos says, "Soon. I will go fishing with you soon."

The room becomes quiet as the main presenters enter with the meeting's organizer.

The subject for tonight is development, and the meeting was called by the town leaders to present plans for a new marina and an expanded airport. Two men, introduced as "developers," are prepared to show drawings and explain how the proposed changes will benefit and bring prosperity to all on Mykonos.

Most Mykoniates, including Elena, believed the controversial expansion plans for the island had been delayed, not to be discussed for at least another year. Everyone was taken by surprise when it was suddenly learned and unexpectedly revealed when Elena returned to the island that the government might approve the plans. No one, not even the mayor, knows the full story on this new, surprising twist.

Before the formal presentation begins, the people talk among themselves.

"The developers want to enlarge the marina and build a larger airport. This will be a major, major expansion for Mykonos."

"It will change our island forever."

"Yes, but is that good or bad?"

"The tourist trade will increase tenfold."

"Will that bring prosperity or trouble or both? I don't know."

Many people see the proposed changes as the next logical step in the growth of the tourist trade and believe it will bring prosperity to all, especially to those willing to sell their land; others oppose the plans because of ecological and environmental concerns. They want the island to be not only for tourists, but for Mykoniates and tourists. The point, they say, is that the island must be shared with discretion.

One of the most developed islands in the Cyclades, Mykonos is small. Its area is only 85 square kilometers with a shoreline of 80 kilometers. The population of Mykonos is a modest 5,500, but at the height of the tourist season, thousands of visitors stay on the island, straining its fragile infrastructure. Mykonos is arid and has very little vegetation. As on most of the islands of the Cyclades, the water supply is limited; many homes are supplied by wells and rainwater collected in cisterns. There is only one sewage plant. It is rare for a home to have a telephone; residents with phones waited years for them to be installed. Most roads on the island are not paved, so the dust created by the mopeds and automobiles is a constant problem.

"Good evening, ladies and gentlemen," Andreas Nomikos, town leader, politician, and organizer, begins. We are here to tell you our plans to bring prosperity to Mykonos. Here are our drawings. This is the new marina, which will accommodate 250 yachts."

"How many yachts can our marina handle now?" a man asks.

"Just twenty-five or thirty, depending upon the size of the vessel," Mr. Nomikos answers.

"What about the windmills?" someone asks.

"The windmills serve no practical function. They must be taken down for the sake of progress," the town leader declares. Shouts of protest begin to fill the room.

Mr. Nomikos quickly moves on to the rest of the plan. He explains that a new airport must be built to accommodate large jet planes from Athens and the rest of Europe.

"Our airport is very small. Only small, propeller-driven planes can land here now," Mr. Nomikos says. He then turns the meeting over to the developers who display their renderings and rapidly make their points in favor of the expansion.

"All of our studies show that it is possible to build a large marina as shown on these drawings," the first developer says, and adds, "The issue here is, are you for progress?"

"There will be a need for more hotels and restaurants and more services," the second developer adds. "People who are forward-thinking will have an opportunity to become wealthy. It is the chance of a lifetime."

"We will all live like kings and queens," Mr. Nomikos interjects.

A young person rises and shouts, "You are not telling everything. In order to build that new marina, you will have to tear down many homes, including those near the windmills!!"

"That is true," the town leader says, "but there will be money to build beautiful new homes in the hills with spectacular views. As for the windmills, remember they serve no practical function. Why keep mere symbols when they stand in the way of great wealth? What is the point?"

The home of Elena's parents is on the Hora port near the windmills. It is a prime location in Mykonos. Elena's parents are not only considering selling, but are excited by the plans and the possibility of a financial windfall.

Elena is vehemently opposed. She has been here before. This is a major source of conflict with her parents. She does not want things to change again. Developers and their plans bring sorrow. She is prepared to fight to prevent this sorrow. Let the present be.

After Mr. Nomikos' comment about the windmills being "mere symbols," the meeting erupts. The group opposing the plan, Elena included, presents its petition.

"This is about our culture," a young man says. "We oppose your plans because it will pollute Mykonos in more ways than one. This plan will destroy the way we live."

"Bah," the town leader says, "you and your friends lack vision. You are not only against progress, you are pretending to be ecologists."

"Why are you playing the role of conservationists?" the first developer asks.

"Romantic idealists," Mr. Nomikos declares. "You are romantic idealists."

The young man and his friends shout:

"Money hungry capitalists!"

"Polluters!"

From the left side of the room, a chant begins: "Save the windmills! Save the windmills!"

"Please, please my friends," Mr. Nomikos pleads, and shouts his slogan: "A new Mykonos for the next millennium!! A new Mykonos for the next millennium!!"

The meeting ends after 9 p.m. The only thing that is clear is that vehement feelings exist on both sides of the issue, and each side remains adamant about how it envisions the future of Mykonos.

Elena's head is spinning. She longs to escape all this and thinks of Matthew's poetry class. When she is on Delos, near Matthew and his students, she finds herself at peace.

Aphrodite's purple cloak lies softly on her shoulders as her golden hair is braided by Eros. Admiring herself, she looks into the mirror she is holding and sees Sappho behind her. "Golden Sister," says Aphrodite, "I am bored, bored, bored!!!"

"I feel your boredom," Sappho responds. "Must we wait for Poseidon? Can't we summon Athena? She likes to assume different forms."

"Athena is going on a boat ride and does not want to be disturbed," Aphrodite says.

"I wish she would stay away from boats and boatmen," Sappho says. Sappho is then suddenly inspired and says, "Let's summon Zephyr, the West Wind."

"Yes, and quickly," Aphrodite commands.

While the town meeting is in progress, Matthew is in his apartment and has just fallen asleep. His windows are open and the night is calm, but suddenly a fierce wind blows; within seconds, papers are whirling around the room and Matthew is awakened. The wind then subsides quickly. "What a strange phenomenon," Matthew thinks, now wide awake.

He rushes to gather his papers, places them safely in his briefcase, then looks about the room to see what is missing. Everything appears to be there. Suddenly, he feels hungry, very hungry. This is strange because he had dinner. Slipping on his light jacket, he decides to go into town for a snack. "Why am I so hungry?" he asks himself.

As he exits the small grocery story with a small bag of snacks, Elena is walking toward him, dressed in white shorts and blouse, her hair fastened atop her head by a barrette. Surprised to see her, Matthew runs his fingers through his thick hair, quickly trying to make it neater than it is. He tucks his rumpled shirt deeper into his slacks.

"Hi," he says, "what brings you to this part of town?"

"The town meeting. I just came from there. The developers want to tear down the windmills. This has me very upset," Elena responds.

"Do you want to go for a walk? Perhaps you will forget about this business for a while?"

"It is very dusty here. Let's go down by the beach. I usually don't like to go there, but it will be very pretty now. The weather is perfect."

"There was a strong wind not too long ago, very strange."

"What wind? You must be mistaken; things have been calm."

"Shall we take a taxi to the beach?" Matthew asks.

"I have my moped. Come on, hop on the back and we'll be there in minutes. I know a shortcut."

Matthew eyes the moped somewhat dubiously. Elena has already started the motor and is waiting for him. He gingerly eases on and holds her tightly around the waist as they race over bumpy, dusty roads to reach a cliff over the beach. Lights from nearby hotels and the brilliance of the moon enable them to follow the path down the side of the cliff to the sea.

"I have never been to this particular spot before," Matthew says. "It's wonderful."

"It is very peaceful here," Elena responds. "Come, take off your shoes and let's walk on the edge of the water," she says, kicking off her sandals.

As they walk along, they see couples on beach chairs, trying to find privacy beneath large umbrellas, and they quickly turn their eyes away. As they pass one chair, Matthew sees his textbook on Sappho on the sand! Brandon and Kallirroi, who are snuggling under their own umbrella, are preoccupied with each other and do not see Matthew and Elena walk by. It is obvious to Matthew, however, that they gave up the pretense of helping each other translate sometime ago!!

The night is calm; the sea and sand on their feet feel wonderful. The evening mist hovers over them as they walk, and small droplets of water dance on them, bringing cool relief. The dew sparkles on Elena's face. She is smiling and Matthew is very relaxed. They hold hands and communicate with lingering glances at each other.

"Do you wear contact lenses?" Matthew asks.

"No, why do you ask?"

"Your eyes are so dark, I thought you must wear tinted contacts. It's so hard to tell nowadays."

They pass the last hotel and turn together to go back because the rest of the beach is dark. The water is lapping at their feet and the moist night air is cool but comfortable.

Halfway up the beach they see two young people walking toward them, holding hands. Matthew and Elena are now absorbed in each other and do not look at them, but Matthew hears, "Good evening Dr. Wyttman," and looks to see Dina and Christos, who are now swinging their arms vigorously and walking apart from each other.

"Hi," Matthew says, a bit startled, "nice night, isn't it?"

"It's a great night," they say, hurrying along.

Matthew and Elena walk slowly along the beach, savoring the night, and are soon at the pathway to the cliff. They gather their shoes and walk up the path. Matthew goes first, holding Elena's hand. When he nears the top, he extends his arm to give Elena a final pull, and as she reaches level ground she throws her arms around Matthew's neck, stands on tiptoe, and kisses him.

He does not exactly return her kiss. "Ah, Elena, Elena," he says, "do you know you are just slightly older than my students?"

Rebuffed, she says, "But you are a young man, you are not ancient!"

"I'm 40," he says. "You are a very young woman. You no doubt think of me as an older man."

"I don't, I don't," she says, "but I certainly am not going to impose myself on you." With that she hops on the moped and prepares to start it.

"Elena, please," Matthew says, "don't go. Look at me." Matthew feels awkward; it has been a long time since he has held a woman and he is a bit unsure of himself.

Elena is sitting backward on the seat with her legs on either side; she suddenly spins around and faces Matthew.

Eros is summoned by Aphrodite and quickly appears, holding his bow and an arrow dipped in a love potion. Eros aims his arrow at Matthew and pulls back on his bow; the arrow hits its mark. Matthew is suddenly emboldened.

He straddles the back wheel and takes her face in both of his hands.

"No one has eyes as deep and dark as yours," he says, bending his face to hers and kissing the dew gently from her lips, slowly and deliberately. He holds her face loosely in his hands as his mouth touches each drop of the sweet moisture. His hands move behind her and he glides his fingers up and down her back, playfully tracing the outlines of the lingerie she is not wearing. Matthew's movements are slow, almost studied, but create an exquisite tension. He pulls her closer to him, kissing her deeply. He does not release her until she needs to breathe. She exhales sharply, but before she can take another breath, his mouth covers hers again. She has never, ever, been kissed like that.

Bending her head back, he moves his lips down her slender neck while his fingers purposely circle the swollen tips of her breasts. Elena's entire body becomes coiled and arched under his feather-like touches, but her emotions are very yielding. This is the effect he sought—spontaneous, overflowing emotions in a tense body. Responding to her, his body becomes taut. They both know they have reached an exquisite peak. But Matthew, wanting to prolong the sensation, continues to move slowly. Elena feels she must not take the lead, but follow him.

To control her passion, she moves away from him slightly and asks, with a slight stutter, "Do...Do you do all things this well?"

Matthew is somewhat surprised by his control, but says calmly, as he continues to stroke her, "I am a fairly good translator."

"That is not what I meant."

"You were not explicit," he says, taking the barrette from her hair.

"Okay," she begins, "do you make…"

But he is determined to maintain the tension. He is still straddling the bike and she is on the seat, facing him. With the tips of his fingers, he traces the outline of her face and her lips, and glides his touch over the downy hair on her arms, sending shivers up her spine. Lifting her, he steps backwards and possessively lowers her down his body, stopping when her warmth covers his. He places his hand on the small of her back and pulls her toward him, saying,

"You burn me."

She murmurs softly as he pulls her closer. Her moisture spills, sticking to him. Inflaming him. Tilting her back, he looks deep into her eyes. He says hoarsely, "Oh, you burn me."

"Did you hear what he said, Aphrodite??" Sappho says, fuming. He said 'You burn me.' He used my words!! He didn't say, 'as Sappho says, You Burn Me,' nor did he say 'I feel the same as Sappho did when she said 'You burn me.' He just said 'You burn me,' without attribution!!!"

"Sappho, Sappho," Aphrodite said, "he said it in the heat of the moment!! You don't attribute words to a poet when they are used in the heat of the moment!!—Did you expect him to stop the love-making and say, 'oh, by the way, the words I will use now are from the great Sappho?"

"It is plagiarism, plagiarism," Sappho rants and raves. "What would my sister Erato, the Muse of love poetry, think?"

"Sappho, your words are universal—they are for everyone."

But there is no soothing Sappho. As she continues to fume, she says, "For this insult I summon Aeolus, the King of the Winds."

Aphrodite pleads with her, but there is no appeasing the Tenth Muse!!

Suddenly, violent winds swirl around Matthew and Elena, blowing sand everywhere and lifting the moped off the ground. The wind is traveling with such force that the sands sting their bodies.

"What in the world is happening?" Elena asks, panting to get her breath.

"Violent winds, violent winds," says Matthew, "they came out of nowhere, just like earlier this evening. Can we make it to the hotel over there?"

"We have to," Elena says, and holding on to each other, they begin to walk down the pathway.

Halfway down the path, the winds subside, just as their passion has subsided.

Down on the beach, Matthew is feeling embarrassed. "My hotel is just down the way a bit. I think I'll head for it now before the winds start again," he says. "Would you like to come with me and I'll get you a taxi from there?"

Elena is equally embarrassed. "No, thank you," she says, "I'll just hop on my moped and make my escape while it is still calm. It will take me just ten minutes to get home."

"Well, goodnight then," Matthew says, "I'll see you soon."

"Yes, goodnight," Elena says.

"By the way," she begins, "where on earth did you learn to—I mean, did you read Ovid's—oh, never mind."

ᘓᘓᘓ

E lena does not have a telephone. Matthew has checked the book and called information, but she is one of the many residents who do not have phones. He did not see her on Delos this morning while teaching, and he is anxious. He does not even know exactly where she lives.

Matthew goes to the taverna where he has seen her and leaves a note with a waitress. He hopes it isn't presumptuous that he has asked her to call him or stop by his flat.

Elena is in the library surrounded by books and lexicons. She was able to find an English translation of Ovid's *The Art of Love*. She reads the entire book slowly and then reads it again. At the end of the afternoon, she is exhausted. She has pages of notes and is smiling coyly.

She wants to see Matthew, but thinks it would be inappropriate to go to his hotel. Besides, Mykonos is a small town and soon everyone will know their business. She has seen him occasionally at a taverna. It is not the one she prefers, but he seems to frequent it. Elena decides to leave a note for him there. In the note, she asks him to meet her by the beach. She tells the waitress that she wants to borrow a book from him. "Would you mind giving him this note?" she asks. "I want to borrow one of his books."

"Of course I will give him your note," the waitress says. "Of course she wants to borrow one of his books," she mutters to herself.

Stephanos, Nikolaos, and Petros are enjoying another peaceful day. They would not have it any other way. As they sailed the seas of Greece on the ferries, their lives were solitary, and with this came peace. Although they would find it difficult to articulate, the need for solitude is a part of their being and has never left their lives.

The retired seafarers are piloting Stephanos' boat to "Big Delos," a nearby island. The boat is stocked with firewood, lanterns, a battery-operated radio, blankets, and other supplies; and their wives have given them sacks of bread, olives, feta cheese, and vegetables. Before reaching "Big Delos," a primitive island where nobody lives, they fish for the catch that will complete their evening meal. They will pull in red mullets, because they know where to find these delicacies.

"Too bad Tassos could not join us," Nikolaos says. "He is so troubled by the development plans. He and Katerina talk about it all the time. They cannot make up their minds."

"There has been enough change on our island already," Petros says, "but let us not dwell on that. We have come here to fish."

Arriving on the island as darkness begins to fall, they prepare a bonfire for light, dig a big hole for another fire where they bake the fish and vegetables, then relax under a brilliant, full moon and drink home-made wine. The moon is so bright, bathing the entire island, that one could read a book by its white light.

"Petros," calls Nikolaos, "play us a song on your *santouri!!*"

"Must I always entertain you?" Petros asks, but he is pleased by his friend's request.

"You play so well, my friend—I swear to the heavens!— please play for us," Nikolaos asks.

Petros holds the ancient instrument, his *santouri*, close to his body, and strums a haunting song. Alone on the island, they sit around the fire, enjoying their wine and anticipating the feast that is slowly cooking on the open fire.

"We will rise early tomorrow to fish and be the first on the quay to sell our catch," Stephanos says. "Petros, if you play those songs on the boat tomorrow, I swear the fish will just jump in."

"The red mullets, maybe," Petros says. "The octopuses are wily creatures and may need some coaxing."

"It is better to be wily, like us," Nikolaos says. "If certain people had thrown their nets over us—and I say this on the grave of my Mother—we would not be fishing now."

"That is true," agrees Stephanos. "We would be meeting with accountants and lawyers, standing behind counters, and rushing to satisfy the whims of the tourists."

"I tried—the Lord is my witness—to learn the ways of business," Petros says.

"Petros, with your thick head you could never understand numbers, only melodies," Nikolaos teases.

"I tried to understand the accountants and lawyers—the devil take my soul if I am not truthful—but when they talked my throat became tight and I could not swallow," Stephanos says.

They were speaking about a time more than twelve years ago when each sold property he owned along the oceanfront and made huge profits. Then, in anticipation of the influx of tourists, they took the advice of family members in Athens, "the men with suits," and purchased restaurants, the lone beer warehouse on the island, plus the ferry service to Delos.

Today, they are among the wealthiest residents of Mykonos. These men do not fish for a living. They fish and sell their catch because they are of the sea. They are Greeks. They are fishermen.

"So my wife and son-in-law are running my business interests," Stephanos says. "That is as it should be. Who ran the family when I was at sea? My wife!!"

"Stephanos is right," Nikolaos agrees. "Our women learned how to be good managers when we were away. And I for one—God will curse me if I lie—I for one am proud of my Maria. It is her good cooking that is served in our hotel and is now being enjoyed by the lucky tourists!!"

"Ah, my friends," Petros says, "as long as we do our share with the businesses on those two feast days, our families will be happy, don't you agree?"

"Yes, yes, and the gods will send their thunder if we don't," Stephanos replies.

The feast days are August 15 and March 25. On these

dates, their wives and extended families go to the nearby island of Tinos, or the "Island of Our Lady," to venerate Mary, the Blessed Virgin. Elaborate ceremonies are held and pilgrims from throughout the world come to Tinos to celebrate. On these feast days, Stephanos, Nikolaos, and Petros tend to business while their wives join the faithful on Tinos.

Petros finishes his songs and carefully places his *santouri* in its case. "Let us eat," he declares.

The food is ready. Each man takes a foil-wrapped package from the fire and carefully opens it, as the aromas from the steamed mullets, small red potatoes, courgettes, and aubergines fill the air. They eat with gusto.

After eating, Stephanos says, "Let's have some bouzouki music on the radio!! Let's dance!!"

Locking their arms in the age-old style of the Greek dancers, the three friends dance, alone on the moon-bathed island.

ᄅᄅᄅ

It is almost daylight. As they doze near each other in sleeping bags, golden Dawn appears, cloaked in a mist. Soft morning clouds are spread over the sky, like strands of damp hair. Inhaling deeply, Dawn begins her cat-like, awakening stretch. Notus, the warm, South wind, exhales, sending a gentle breeze over the three fishermen.

The men awaken and prepare for the return journey. The sea is calm. They pilot the boat to Stephanos' favorite spot where the hungry fish always bite.

Near a secret cove, about halfway to Mykonos, Stephanos stops the boat, and the three men fish. Stephanos, Nikolaos, and Petros do not have fishing poles.

They do not have boxes of bait. Dropping a net to catch the first fish, they slice it for bait and attach the bait to a simple hook. They fish with the line resting gently on weathered and callused index fingers. They need nothing more.

DIDO   AENEAS   CLAIRE   ARGOS   SAPPHO   DIONYSUS

Across the sea in Greenwich, London, it is 12:58 p.m. The red ball on the top of the Old Royal Observatory, which sits like a crown on the highest hill in Greenwich Park, begins its slow ascent to the top of a long pole on the building's dome. At exactly 1 p.m., the ball drops silently and without fanfare. A practice ordered by the Admiralty in 1833 to give seamen on the Thames a visual time check, it continues to this day.

Although no longer the country's principal observatory, it attracts thousands of international visitors annually who come to see this architectural masterpiece designed by Sir Christopher Wren. Tourists visit the observatory also for the experience of straddling both hemispheres on the prime meridian line, or longitude zero, which separates the eastern and western hemispheres and runs through

Greenwich. Visitors standing astride this line delight in having their pictures taken with one foot in the East and the other in the West.

Dr. Claire Billington is in her stately lime-washed home at No. 3 The Paragon in Blackheath, a village on a plateau above Greenwich, when the ball falls. She happened to put down her knitting and check her watch at exactly 1 p.m. In another hour or so, she will place a phone call to Matthew in Greece and explain the problems that have arisen over the Senior Lectureship. In the meantime, she plans to take Matthew's bulldog, Argos, for a walk in Greenwich Park. The scarf she is knitting for Matthew as a surprise Christmas present will be completed at another time.

Matthew's "faithful dog" loves his daily walk in the park, but to reach it from Claire's house they must cross the Heath. Claire notices that Argos almost always races over this area, even though his short legs have to work very hard to maintain a fast pace. Today as the brindle pup pulls her along the Heath, she thinks she hears him growl.

The weather is a bit strange. It appears as though a storm is about to develop, then suddenly the winds die down and the sky brightens. Claire looks at the sky, shrugs, and continues on her walk.

Various rumors about the Heath have circulated for years. The most persistent rumor is that it is an ancient burial ground, even though no excavation has ever unearthed bones. Some say thousands of people who died during the Black Deaths in the fourteenth century are buried there. Others have said bodies buried there are those of the Danes who invaded the area in 1011, but nothing has been proven.

It is a fact, however, that Watling Street, the Roman road leading from Dover to Rochester and into London, crossed

Blackheath. Armies traveled it and fought battles there. A spur ran diagonally west from Shooters Hill toward what was possibly a small Roman temple in Greenwich Park, passing the site of the present Royal Standard public house.

Through the centuries the Heath has been the setting of many turbulent historical events. It has served as a rallying point for troops marching on London. Roman legions crossed it on their way to London. The Danes camped there in the eleventh century, and, during the Peasants' Revolt in 1381, Wat Tyler and his supporters bravely assembled to meet Richard II.

Spectacular events have also brought crowds to the Heath. Thousands came to cheer the victorious Henry V on his return from Agincourt in 1415. A great pageant was staged for Anne of Cleeves when she arrived to marry Henry VIII. And excitement was high in May 1660 when 120,000 people and the army waited to greet the bare-headed Charles II as he rode across the Heath on his way into London at the Restoration of the Monarchy.

It is not difficult to envision troops marching, protesters assembling, and royals engaging in pageantry on these grounds, because the very grandeur of the Heath invites events of epic proportion. It seduces modern day visitors with its mysteriousness and its lofty magnificence, just as it must have held allure for the throngs in centuries past. Most of its secrets, however, belong to history.

The Heath is what is known as "common land"; its 270 acres acquired for the people of London in 1871 by an Act of Parliament. Like Hampstead Heath and other open spaces, the land is inalienable and no one is permitted to build houses or to otherwise encroach upon it.

Today there are no royals or peasants on the Heath. Just a Professor of Classics and a little bulldog, who walk quickly over this historical terrain, approaching the entrance to Greenwich Park. Argos resumes a normal pace and waits calmly for Claire to remove his leash. She had scolded him yesterday for being impatient when she tried to unlock his leash, and he had shown his resentment by tugging at her knitting that night. But he is friendly and obedient this morning, and Claire is pleased that he does not hold a grudge.

Well-behaved dogs are allowed to play freely in the park, and since a well-trained and obedient dog is a status symbol in England, it is rare to see dogs attack each other or hear them bark or growl. It is almost as though the dogs have made a pact to get along and share the 200-acre park. Claire removes the leash, and Argos stands quietly surveying the park before racing for his favorite chestnut tree.

Claire walks slowly up the tree-lined path near the pavilion where various community bands present lively concerts on Sundays during the summer. She stops near a bench where an elderly woman sits, throwing crumbs of bread to the squirrels and the occasional bird who dares to venture near the small, scurrying animals. Argos runs about, carefully ignoring the other dogs, then rushes to Claire and seeks her approval for his gentlemanly behavior.

Claire is pleased with Argos and stops to pet him as he stands politely before her, panting and shaking from side to side.

"Lovely dog," the woman on the bench says. "What is his name?"

"Argos."

"Ah, Argos," the woman says, petting him.

"Only God could love you for yourself alone, and not your darling wrinkles."

"That's precious," Claire says appreciatively. "Argos thanks you."

"Tell him it is Billy Yeats he should be thanking," the woman laughs.

"Ah, yes," says Claire and motions for Argos to follow her along the path to the far end of the park where more of his favorite chestnut trees await him.

Greenwich Park is the oldest of London's royal parks. Medieval documents describe it as a royal hunting ground near a "great house by the river," sometimes called Bella Court, where Henry V's brother, Humphrey Duke of Gloucester, lived. The main section of the house was destroyed in 1500, and the bricks were used in the new palace that Henry VII built on the waterfront. This became Placentia, the favorite palace of Henry VIII and Elizabeth I.

In 1605 King James gave Greenwich Park with all its houses and lodges to his Danish wife, Queen Anne. She commissioned the famous architect, Inigo Jones, to build the elegant Queen's House, one of the park's modern day attractions. It sits majestically on the bottom grounds in a direct line with the Old Royal Observatory, built in 1675 by order of King Charles II.

಄಄಄

This is Matthew's world. He lives at the bottom of the park in a former carriage house on Feather's Place, directly off Park Vista. It is a convenient and quiet location for him. His favorite pub, The Plume of Feathers, is nearby, and he is a short walk from the Maze Hill rail station where he takes the train daily for the twenty-minute ride into London.

Claire, on the other hand, lives atop the park to the south of the Old Royal Observatory in fashionable

Blackheath with its elegant Victorian homes and trendy shops. Her home is just off the Heath, to the left of the stately Clarendon Hotel, and the popular Princess of Wales Pub, named after Caroline, the wife of the Prince Regent who lived in the area in the early nineteenth century. This pub is the weekend meeting place for London's rising young professionals who come to fly kites or watch soccer games played on the Heath.

Claire had tried to persuade Matthew to live in Blackheath. "The SE 3 postal code is very desirable," she said.

But Matthew prefers the less pretentious Greenwich, postal code SE 10. It is convenient to live near Claire, however, because he is protective of Argos and can always count on Claire to look after the pup when he is away.

Matthew will see Argos sooner than he planned. When Claire finally telephones him in Greece, she convinces him that he has to return at once before the committee on promotions makes a recommendation on the Senior Lectureship. The committee has been meeting informally during the Long Vacation, but Claire senses that a problem is developing.

⠿⠿⠿

Matthew is frantic. He has not been able to talk with Elena.

"I must see her, I must," he says and decides to try to find her studio by the windmills.

Mykonos is a small town. The first person he sees by the windmills directs him to Elena's place. She is sitting outside, sketching. As soon as she sees him, they embrace.

"I left a note for you at the taverna," Matthew begins.

"But I was not there, because I left a note for you at the other taverna."

"We are star-crossed," Matthew says.

"Not if I can help it," Elena says.

"Come in, I will make some tea and we can talk," she offers.

"Elena, the reason I'm so desperate to see you is that I have to leave for Athens right now on the next ferry. I hope to get a seat on a chartered flight from Athens to Heathrow. It's easier to arrange this in London than in Athens."

"Whatever is the matter?"

"There is a problem at university and I have to sort it out. I will return as soon as I can," he explains. "I wanted you to know that."

"Are you trying to tell me you no longer think you are too old for me?" she asks.

"Something like that," he responds.

"I'm playing a game of minutes," Matthew says. "I have to take a cab to the ferry. I'll be back early Wednesday afternoon. Wait for me on the quay, if you can."

"I will," Elena says. "I will wait for you on the quay."

⌂⌂⌂

In Athens, he is able to find a canceled seat on a charter flight. The ticket agent is a bit taken aback by his knowledge of charter cancellations and his fluency in Greek. As the plane leaves Athens, the weather is clear, and he looks forward to a good flight.

Sappho and Aphrodite are in a flutter. Poseidon cannot be found. They thought there were signs he was up and about, but he is probably hiding in his splendid palace at the bottom of the sea. Without Poseidon, they cannot prevent Matthew from leaving. They have worn out their welcome with Aeolus, King of the Winds.

"Come, Aphrodite, let us rest awhile, but bring your servant, Eros, and we will drink nectar from jeweled goblets before we sleep," Sappho says.

Matthew arrives in Greenwich in the early evening, but decides he will wait until morning to call Claire. It was a long trip and he needs to relax. After he unpacks, he leaves his flat on Feather's Place and walks around the corner to The Plume of Feathers pub.

Frequented by locals, the Plume attracts a steady clientele of regulars. No loud music is ever heard in the Plume and because people can hear each other speak, spirited conversation flows freely. It is an old-fashioned, authentic pub.

Occasionally, some tourists coming to Greenwich to visit the Old Royal Observatory, the magnificent Royal Navy Academy and Maritime Museum, and the Cutty Sark clipper will happen upon The Plume by chance. These fortunate visitors have the distinction of discovering one of the best pubs in Southeast London.

Men who are "the regulars" come in singly to sit at the bar and sip their pints. Couples and groups share seats by the wall on comfortable benches and chairs, placing their drinks on small tables between the seats. This arrangement places people in warm proximity to each other. With shoulders sometimes touching and conversations easily overheard, no one is a stranger for long.

There are comfortable outdoor patios to the side and in the back. Tables and benches are shaded by large, colorful umbrellas. It is in these pleasant gardens that family members usually sit with their children and dogs after walks in the park. The pub has a wholesome, friendly atmosphere. People come for this as well as the excellent food.

Daily luncheon specials usually include homemade Shepherd's Pie and lasagna, with the ubiquitous Ploughman's Lunch. Excellent pasta dishes and salmon dinners are prepared fresh and served in the evenings by a couple who once owned a major marketing firm, but left it to become caterers because of their passion for cooking. Because of the couple's culinary skills, The Plume has a loyal following of dinner patrons.

In previous years, one evening a week was devoted to cooking seafood and steaks on a grill for a weekly barbecue advertised as happening "Rain or Shine." This practice was discontinued, but many patrons are lobbying for its return.

The Plume of Feathers was established in 1691 in the reign of William and Mary. The original building had several outbuildings and stables for livestock. It was owned through the years by a number of widows; by a man who eventually entered an asylum; and by persons from various trades, including a master mariner, a fishmonger, a plasterer, and a tailor. The pub also changed hands through

CUSTOMERS   PAN   ARGOS   SAPPHO   DIONYSUS

numerous breweries, and the present day owner is Watney Brewery. Every Wednesday the owners sponsor "Quiz Night."

"Good evening, Matthew," a voice says as Matthew sits on an end stool, "will you be trying your luck with our questions tonight?" It is Fred, the Quiz Master, sitting behind Matthew in front of his small microphone and sorting through stacks of paper that he will soon distribute.

"Hello, Fred," Matthew responds. "How have you been? Gone sailing in Rochester lately?"

"Not recently. The waters have been too choppy."

"I know about choppy seas."

"Can I sign you up for Quiz Night?"

"I don't think I'm going to play tonight. I wasn't able to answer a single question last time for your quiz on rock music."

"You mean you didn't know the names of the sweet, even-tempered Gallagher brothers in the group, Oasis? You didn't know who wrote the lyrics, 'uh, uh, uh, uh, stayin' alive, stayin' alive?' You didn't know what songs were made popular by the American group, Hootie and the Blowfish?"

"Afraid not," Matthew laughs.

Amused, the Quiz Master says, "Tonight may be more to your liking."

Dave, the barman, approaches and asks Matthew if he is going to have a Ruddles County or an Old Speckled Hen.

"A pint of County please, Dave," Matthew says, "and how have you been? What's new?"

"As you can imagine, everyone is talking about the dome they're building down by the Thames for the Millennium celebration. It's going to be the world's largest. People say you'll be able to fit two Wembley stadiums or 13 Albert Halls into it," Dave says.

"Yes, I've been following stories about the construction. What will be inside?"

"The Millennium Committee says it's going to be a surprise, but I expect there will be live performances and exhibitions. Probably an international food court, from what I hear."

Matthew says, "It will probably change Greenwich forever."

"I know there will be some changes the first year," Dave says. "They are expecting 12 million visitors here."

"Wow. I'll have a pint on that," Matthew declares, looking at the beer taps. "I see you're still keeping the mates happy with the best real ale in London. But don't I see a tap for Guinness?"

"That's for the tourists," Dave laughs.

The delights of drinking real ale and the state of the British brewing industry just happen to be the favorite topics of conversation for the mates at the bar. They soon join the conversation:

"Ruddles County is a good-bodied beer, but I like the hoppy flavor and dry finish of Ruddles Best Bitter."

"Remember Marston's Pedigree Bitter? Well, Marston has now produced a sulphurous India Pale Ale—brewing at its best!"

"The India Pale Ale is popular as a guest beer in many a tavern."

"I hear on bank holidays mates are taking the Eurostar to France and coming back with vans filled with beer."

"That's a fact. A bloke can bring back as much beer as his van can carry. Pay only one-seventh of the duty we pay. The French pay about four pence tax and we pay thirty!! May be worth a trip through the chunnel to stock up, mates!!"

"Can't get a top-up on the other side of the channel, I'll wager. If the pint comes with an inch of foam, too bad. At least here a pint of beer equals a pint of liquid!"

A vendor selling fresh snacks from a box strapped around his neck enters and circulates among the patrons. "Fresh cockles, fresh cockles," he sings.

A woman with a tin is circulating, also, asking for donations for a charity for the elderly.

People check their watches and hurry to their places.

Fred, the Quiz Master, finally announces: "Last chance to enter Quiz Night. Just a quid a person. No more than six to a team. Tonight we have six categories with twelve questions in each. Sorry, I cannot announce the categories beforehand. Top team wins gift certificates for dinners and/or the good old 'Rain or Shine Barbecue' if we can ever get it back!"

Matthew opts not to participate in Quiz Night. He prefers to sit alone with his pint of Ruddles County and enjoy the atmosphere. He is always amused and entertained by the questions asked by the Quiz Master.

His thoughts are on Elena. He knows that he has entered untested waters and feels excited. He's surprised that he is excited. The choices he has made in his life have always been safe. A teacher and a translator. Essentially, always his own man. After all, how many people can challenge him on his translations of ancient Greek documents. "Now that I think about it," Matthew ruminates, "why would anyone bother to read some of those works?"

He knows Elena is a passionate woman. It is in her very being. It is in her country. She is Greek. Matthew knows that he is British to the core. He can show emotion, but that goes against form. He remembers an American friend explaining her surprise at a particular incident. She watched people from the U.K. stand patiently in line as an inconsiderate tourist buying a ticket made everyone late for an incoming train by asking a host of questions of the ticket master. "What would you have expected to see?" Matthew asked her. "Well, in America," she replied, "we would have shouted at him and told him to get to the end of the line." "Now that would be very bad form, wouldn't it?" Matthew remembered replying.

Still ruminating, Matthew is thinking, "I am passionate. I have been passionate about my work." Then he reminds himself that he is, after all, a man of reason, and a man can't take a manuscript to bed now, can he, and whoever saw a manuscript with eyes so dark and deep?

He wonders how he will be able to concentrate on the business of the Senior Lectureship tomorrow. It seems so unimportant now.

Pub patrons take Quiz Night seriously. Some determined contenders for prizes are known to participate regularly in Quiz Nights in various pubs throughout London, traveling far and wide to Bloomsbury, Hampstead Heath, North Wembley, Hammersmith, Seven Sisters, Blackfriars, Piccadilly Circus, Shepherd's Bush, and even Deptford.

After all teams have signed up, Fred announces, "Tonight, mates, our quiz is on Greek mythology."

"A storm woke me up last night and I had a sudden inspiration to include this category," Fred continues, "so I went into my files and some interesting questions popped up."

A group of four players sits behind Matthew. Every team must pick a name and these men are the "A Team."

"Wonder if any questions on poetry popped up?" one man on A Team says to one of his three companions.

"Right," his friend says, "what was that poem you got right last time? You had to know the second line. What was the first line?"

"Who could forget Shakespeare's 'Shall I compare thee to a summer's day?'"

"The quiz master asked for the second line. What was that?"

"'Rough winds do shake the darling buds of May.'"

"Indeed, 'rough winds do shake the darling buds of May.' Lovely image, that."

"Here we go, mates, a quiz on Greek mythology," Fred begins. "First question. Who is the Tenth Muse?"

The A Team ponders this question, speaking quietly among themselves.

"It is a poetess, but I cannot recall her name."

DIONYSUS AND SAPPHO

A clap of lightening and a roll of thunder disturb the calm atmosphere in the Plume and startle the patrons as they ask each other, "What was that?"

A member of the A Team says quickly, "My wife said never call a woman poet a poetess. She said a poet is a poet is a poet."

"Is your wife a feminist?"

"You'll have to ask her," the man says. "God knows I would never speak for her!!"

"Ah, she's a feminist," his mate says.

Matthew, much amused, is smiling broadly.

"Second question," Fred says. "How did Penelope occupy her time as she waited for Odysseus?"

"I remember that from reading the ancients. She knitted. We used to say, 'That's going to be a mighty big scarf.' That bloke, Odysseus, was gone twenty years. And she knitted all that time!!"

"Number three," says Fred. "What is the name of Odysseus' dog?"

"Oh, it is on the tip of my tongue," one of the players says as Matthew gets up to go to the loo.

Putting his hand to the side of his mouth, Matthew whispers to the A Team, "Try Argos."

During the time it takes Matthew to walk to the loo and back, he hears Fred ask three more questions.

"What is a favorite way for goddesses to make their presence known to humans?"

"In mythology, when a famous person died, he or she sometimes took the form of a bright object in the sky. What is this bright object?"

"Where was the god Apollo born?"

Matthew happily tells himself the answers to the three questions.

"A goddess made her presence known by appearing in a brilliant flash, a famous person sometimes took the form of a star, and Apollo was born under an olive tree on Delos."

Returning to his seat at the end of the bar, Matthew hears Fred ask, "Who is Aphrodite?"

"I know that," the player says. "She is the goddess of love."

"Are you sure that is her name? I thought it was Venus."

"Question eight," Fred says. "Who is the god of the Vine or the god of Wine?"

"Bacchus," the player says, "I know Bacchus is the god of wine."

"Ah ha," the other man says, "that's the Roman god. Fred is trying to trick us. This quiz is on Greek mythology. The Greek god is Dionysus."

"Right, right," says the second man, "and the Greek goddess of love is Aphrodite, not Venus."

Seeing Matthew smile, the men ask him his opinion and he says, "I think you have it all figured out. Keep up the good work."

"Next question," Fred says. "Who are the three women in mythology who always dance together, spreading mirth and good cheer?"

"Three women, three women," the man ponders, "I can't think of the names of three women who danced together. Maybe one was Ginger. Maybe that is how Ginger Rogers got her name."

"Be serious," the other player says.

"Question 10," Fred announces. "This is in two parts, but you get only one point."

A long groan fills the Plume.

"What is the name of the woman who was abducted by a young prince called Paris, and what famous war was then fought to rescue the woman Paris carried away?"

"I know that," the man on the A Team says. "The woman is Helen and the war was The Trojan War."

"Eleven," Fred says. "What did the sirens do to seduce Odysseus and delay his return?"

"I think they fed him flowers," the player says, "That's how they got the name lotus eaters. Write 'they fed him flowers.'"

"That's not right," the other player says. "They were sirens, so they sang songs to delay him."

"Last question in this category," Fred announces. "Legend says the poet Sappho died by throwing herself into the sea from a cliff on the Island of Leucas. What is this method of suicide called?"

"He saves the toughest for the last," the player says. "Anyone know the answer?"

"Try cliff hanger," his mate says.

Fred asks the teams to bring their answers to him and he takes a few minutes to assign points, then announces the correct answers.

Cheers and jeers fill the pub as Fred reads the questions, then the correct answers. The jeers are the loudest when he says, "Finally, the answer to question twelve about Sappho's suicide is 'the Leucadian Leap.'"

"I ask you, mates," the player says, "now who would know the answer to that? What do you think, governor?" he asks Matthew.

"It's certainly not the most useful knowledge, is it?" Matthew responds.

Savoring his last pint, Matthew waits until all categories are finished and the winners are announced. The A Team scored highest and won the prize. Soon the first bell rings, signaling closing time. Customers can sit for twenty minutes more consuming their ale, then at 11 the pub closes. Matthew is now pleasantly mellow. Quiz night is always fun, and it helps him to relax before the next day's meeting with Claire.

"Goodnight, Fred, take care of that sailboat," Matthew says.

"Goodnight, Governor," Fred says. "Happy sailing to you, too."

Last night at the pub and this morning, as he gets ready to go to university, his thoughts are on Elena. He can see her eyes and face and feel her warmth. He wonders what she is doing and if she thinks of him.

ᕹᕹᕹ

E lena does not tire of riding her moped to the cliff and walking along the beach. She likes to come here now that Matthew is gone, walking slowly up and down the beach and practicing her asanas on the cliff. She stays there for hours, reasoning that she has to do her practice *somewhere*. The time spent by the beach extends her joy and keeps her memories of Matthew close to her.

She knows that most of the time, Matthew is reserved. "He is not of the Mediterranean," she reasons, and, for her, that explains it all. She does not have to ruminate.

Elena wants Matthew to love her. She wonders if she is too young for him. "No, I will be a new experience for him," she thinks. She would like to see him relax more. "Yes, I will take him to see Greek dancing," she muses. She is in love. She is an optimist.

Matthew makes his way to his office at the university. Claire is finishing her class before her meeting with him and is explaining the next assignment.

"I would like you to write in your personal voice," she tells the students. "We have just examined the story of Odysseus. Consider what that means to you."

"Ask yourself," Claire continues. "Can you relate to Odysseus' tribulations, his battles, his assumption of personal responsibility, his coping skills, his relationships with women, for example?"

Matthew passes her classroom and hears the assignment. He shakes his head in exasperation. "What is happening to standards?" he asks himself.

Matthew waits in Claire's office; she comes there directly after class. He is admiring her collection of Greek urns arranged two by two on her bookshelves and he tells her so.

"One good urn deserves another!" Claire declares, relating to Matthew in her usual style of a witty barb. This seems to lessen the delicate tension between them.

Claire comes right to the point. "As I explained on the telephone," Claire says, "your promotion to Senior Lectureship may be in jeopardy."

"Why?" asks Matthew.

"Because," Claire explains, "the promotions committee has begun to talk about other candidates for this position to 'balance' the department. Some think we have too many traditional scholars and that we need some fresh approaches. There is a concern that our department is becoming stale."

She urges him to allow her to lobby the faculty on his behalf. She says many of them are gone during the Long Vacation, but she can reach some of them. The others are here. She says she sees members of the promotions committee often.

Matthew hesitates. He is grateful for her support, but thinks it unseemly to plot and strategize.

"I don't see how I can lobby them, Claire," Matthew says.

"Why?" she asks.

"You know them as well as I do," he replies. "And after all, Claire," Matthew says, "this is not a vote for a Master of a Cambridge college."

"Agreed," Claire replies, "but surely you know that I will do a 'masterful job' of rounding up the votes if you give me permission to take the lead."

He demurs, but to keep her support he says, "I must think about it."

Matthew agrees with her that it was important for him to return at this time and circulate among his colleagues, but he is loath to lobby. He thinks that by spending the next

several days in the department and interacting with his colleagues, he will reaffirm that his interest in the position is
still keen.

"Matthew, I think you must be more aggressive."

"I'm not convinced. Claire, I really should be concentrating on my translations, and that is a bit more difficult
than playing the psychologist."

"Whatever do you mean?"

Matthew explains that he passed her door as she gave
the assignment to her students to write about their feelings
and use the "personal voice."

"I find this approach relevant and refreshing," Claire
declares.

"Really, Claire, we must uphold our standards. After all,
we are British."

Claire smiles in amusement. "Some of our colleagues
will be in their offices tomorrow. Why don't you stop by
then and have a word? I know for a fact that Collins,
Anderson, and Pennypacker will be here and perhaps a few
others."

"I'll do that," Matthew says. "I wanted to talk with Collins
anyway—haven't talked to him in awhile."

"May I stop at your home once more to see Argos before
I leave?" he asks.

"Of course," Claire says happily.

᠅᠅᠅

Many of the academic staff take advantage of the
summer break to go on holiday, but a few dedicated souls remain in their college rooms, engrossed in
their work. When Matthew returns the next morning, he goes
first to his office and then strolls down the long corridor to
see his colleagues.

The door to Collins' office is open and Matthew peers in over his glasses. Collins, whose thick grey hair touches the collar of his flannel shirt, sits with his back to the door, carefully sorting stacks of index cards and moving the stacks around on his desk. Bright red braces, attached to his baggy trousers, hang loosely over his shoulders. Matthew sees that he is wearing a headset and then notices the CD cover for Verdi's *La Traviata*.

The last time he came to Collins' office, Collins was listening to *Die Meistersinger*, and he did not disturb him then as he will not disturb him now. Matthew knows that it is Collins' habit, when he is concentrating on one of the numerous languages in which he is fluent, to listen to opera in that language.

"He's moved from his German phase to his Italian phase," Matthew thinks to himself as he turns away and walks down the corridor. "Oh well, I'll pop in later," he thinks.

He wonders if Claire remembers the last time someone from the department actually spoke with Collins.

Anderson is in her office and, seeing Matthew, gives him a hearty welcome and invites him in.

"Come in, Wyttman, come in," she says. "I have so many questions to ask you about Greece."

It amuses Matthew that it was Dr. Beryl Anderson who began the practice of addressing both men and women on the academic staff by their surnames and that everyone then readily adopted this habit. Matthew thought it was her way of reminding herself, and everyone else, of her Cambridge days.

As Matthew takes a seat, she begins, "I had a lovely invitation to attend a seminar next week in Paris, but of course I cannot go and you will understand why.

"Just look at my *Amorphophallus rivieri*," she says, pointing proudly to the foot-tall plant near the window.

Matthew begins, "Your Amorpho—really, Anderson!!"

"Oh, Wyttman," Anderson chides, "don't be such a prude!! As you can see, the flowers have started to come up, haven't they? Since it blooms just once a year, I said to myself, 'Beryl, you cannot possibly attend that seminar, can you? In three weeks the flowers will be another foot tall and if you are in Paris you will miss it all!!'"

Anderson continues, "The bloom, which you know, Wyttman, takes on a lovely pink iridescent sheen with a dark maroon in its interior, is not to be missed!! Just once a year it blooms, once a year!! Such an exotic flower. It makes me quite cross when people call it 'The Devil's Tongue' or 'The Voodoo Lily.' One should always call a flower by its proper name, don't you agree? Ah, well, today people know little Latin and less Greek.

"What do you say to that, Wyttman, people know little Latin and less Greek?

"I say, Wyttman, what have you been up to?" she continues. "You must come with me to the Chelsea Flower Show in late May. It's a brilliant thing to do. The show's bedazzling, simply bedazzling. The Queen Mother never misses it. Last year she brought the Queen along. I saw them having tea in the garden!! The blooms are choice, simply choice. The Royal Horticultural Society never fails us serious gardeners. You'll enjoy it, Wyttman. Do as I do. Take your portable garden chair, a copy of Vergil, and read in the shade of the chestnut tree!"

Matthew interjects, "You've certainly planted a seed, Anderson. I'll put it on my calendar for next May. I suppose I must be going now."

"So soon? Well, lovely talking with you. And, Wyttman...," she begins.

"Yes," Matthew pauses, thinking he may have an opportunity to change the subject.

"Enjoy Greece. Don't be like me—I fear Greeks bearing gifts!! Do you like that Wyttman? I fear Greeks bearing gifts?"

Shaking his head as he moves along, Matthew sees Pennypacker bounding up the hall.

"Wyttman, old boy, how are you?" Pennypacker bellows. "Pop into my office and tell me about Greece."

When Matthew enters he sees a new collection of posters in Pennypacker's office. Large pictures of Egypt's Sphinx and Pyramids are on the wall next to the skin of a zebra and a variety of African masks.

Pennypacker begins, "Those young editors at Daedalus have been hounding me for more articles on Pindar. Won't let me rest, ole chap. I'm a perfectionist, you know that, Wyttman. I ask myself if I should share my new ideas with those young Turks. They will bloody well steal them. I submit an article and the next thing I know my idea turns up in a dissertation!! Before the article is bloody published, mind you!!! The swine!! Why should I throw pearls before swine? Right, Wyttman?

"Did I tell you, Wyttman, I am now studying Gulf Arabic. A little diversion—an avocation of mine. Actually, a big diversion from my main scholarship. As you know, I am known throughout the world for my articles on the Pindaric odes. Getting to like Gulf Arabic though. Quite fluent, actually. Interested in the Sphinx and the Pyramids. Those New Agers started me on a new path again. A few years ago these same New Agers tried to place the cradle of civilization in Africa!! Had to settle that problem!! Remember that? Ah, the burden of knowledge!! I wish I could concentrate on my Latin and Greek. What a luxury that would be!!

"Now these crystal gazers are trying to prove the Sphinx does not belong to Egypt, but was built by an older civilization 12,000 years ago!! They say they had solid evidence, but it has suddenly gone missing. Gone missing, mind you!! Bloody rot!! But someone has to prove them wrong, right, Wyttman? I'm going to take a look at the hieroglyphs. I'll have a go at the Great Sphinx of Giza!! What do you think of that, Wyttman?"

"A colossal undertaking," Matthew says, rising to leave, "and rather enigmatic."

"Must you go already, old chap?" Pennypacker asks. "Always nice talking to you and learning what you're up to!! Thanks for popping in."

Matthew heads for the common room at the end of the hallway. As he approaches the door, he hears feminine voices and the phrase "deconstructing."

"Oh, no," Matthew says, coming to a full stop.

"Of course, there is a difference between feminism and feminist criticism," a voice says.

"Yes, and there is a difference between reexamining and deconstructing the text," another voice declares.

Feeling a bit deconstructed himself, Matthew leaves.

ⴰⴰⴰ

That evening back at Greenwich, Matthew takes a leisurely walk along the river's edge to Ballast Quay Way and sits on a bench in front of the Cutty Sark Pub. It is two years since he last walked this way. The pub is in a secluded corner of Greenwich that few tourists discover. At night, it is even more difficult to find because one has to walk down poorly lighted, twisted alleyways to reach it.

The Cutty Sark is very old, and although it had been rebuilt several times because of fires, there had been a pub on the Ballast Quay since 1695. Ships docked there to unload their cargoes and then filled their empty ships with gravel or ballast to weigh them down for the journey to collect more cargo. Matthew appreciates the area's maritime history and can almost feel the ghosts of old seamen passing by.

As he sits on the bench at the Cutty Sark looking through the mist at the Isle of Dogs across the river in Docklands, loud rock music blares from the pub; it rattles his nerves. He had never heard rock music in an English pub before. It simply isn't done.

"Barbarians," he thinks and promises himself he will read a book recommended to him called *Death of the British Pub.*

"One more tradition slipping away," he mutters.

He is thinking about Elena. "She is so beautiful and young and so full of life," he muses. "In a short time she will tire of me. How can I match her vitality?"

ᛝᛝᛝ

Elena is in her apartment, listening to songs by Anna Vissi and dancing by herself. She is thinking about Matthew. "He is so mature and focused," she ruminates. "How can I keep his interest?"

ᛝᛝᛝ

Before leaving for the airport the next morning, Matthew goes to Claire's home to say goodbye to her and to Argos. Claire is expecting him, and when he knocks she quickly hides her knitting and goes to fetch the pup.

"Can you stay for a cuppa? Did you talk to Collins and Anderson? How about Pennypacker?"

"In answer to your first question, sorry, I am really pressed for time and don't have time for tea, but thanks. My flight to Athens leaves in a few hours."

"And my second question?" Claire persists.

"I don't know how to answer that. Let's say they talked to me."

"Well, what did they say?"

"The usual, the usual."

"You are so exasperating!" Claire says. "I'll talk to them, if you don't mind."

"Good luck," Matthew says. "Now let me say goodbye to the pup." He calls, "Here Argos, here Argos."

But Argos remains at his favorite spot near the fireplace and pretends to ignore Matthew.

SAPPHO   APHRODITE   EROS

A rare night off becomes a reality for Yannis; he dresses carefully in freshly pressed light blue trousers and a white t-shirt. He pressed the clothes himself so his attire would be perfect. He feels lighthearted and happy; tonight is his and he will enjoy it in the Mykonos Bar. Even though he worked hard all day, now there is an extra bounce in his already buoyant step. He is exuding what the Greeks call *kefi*, a good, happy mood. Tonight he is filled with *kefi*. Tonight, he will dance.

He hears the soulful sounds of the Rhembetika music before he enters and smiles broadly, thinking of the release he will feel when he begins to dance. Rhembetika music was first brought to Greece in 1922 following the Asia Minor Catastrophe, when more than a million Greeks were massacred and forced from their homelands in Smyrna and other areas of the Asia Minor coast. Many settled in Athens and composed plaintive, wailing laments about their exile and lost homeland. This style of music, which was said "to come from the bowels," became known as Rhembetika.

Yannis stands still, allowing the music to fill his senses. His body and emotions are taut and he feels tightly coiled. He suppresses an impulse to spin into the room as if he were a top, leaving his troubles behind him on a thin string.

For many Greeks, dancing is part of living. There are hundreds of distinctive Greek dances. Some are performed at festivals to mark specific religious holidays, and others are designed to express intensive emotions. Greek tourists and natives of Mykonos understand this and gather at the Mykonos Bar to express themselves through dance.

Inside, the room is dark and smoky and the music loud. To the left of the bar is a small lounge with a padded sofa that curves against the wall, and to the right is a crowded dance floor. Some people are actually dancing, while others are simply standing and talking and gesturing broadly. Two tiers of tables, arranged stadium style, surround the dance floor.

Yannis notices that the crowd seems to be watching dancers at the far end of the floor, and he maneuvers to get a better look. He sees Elena, dancing the *tsifte-teli* with girlfriends. The *tsifte-teli* is a very expressive, graceful, shuffling type of movement slightly reminiscent of the belly-dance, and has its origins in the Eastern influence in Asia Minor. With light steps, Elena sways first to her right, then to her left, her hips and arms moving in quick, lyrical movements. Her feet quickly close, one passes in front of the other, then one passes behind the other, but those watching are not conscious of the footwork because Elena has created a complete picture, a lovely image, a distinctive sensation. Her body says, "Life is Good." Her slender hips, her graceful arms, and her infectious smile say, as she sways, "Yes, Life is Good."

The live music is played by the Zygia, a group of musicians using various combinations of the clarinet, violin, lute, and *santouri*. Tonight, a tambourine accompaniment and drums will enhance the music, depending upon what compositions they play. The song ends and the dancers walk over a floor of carnations to find their seats.

Yannis is waiting for Elena, who is surprised to see him.

"What, no work tonight?" she asks, breathless, still happy from her dancing.

"Night off, night, off," Yannis explains, guiding her by the arm to the lounge. "Elena, we must talk," he pleads.

"You have a night off and you want to talk! Yannis, let's dance."

"Don't tease me, Elena."

"I am not teasing. You are my favorite dancer. You are the best and you know it."

"Just your favorite dancer, am I? What happened to favorite man? Elena, in my home in Northern Greece—" Yannis begins.

"Listen, they are playing a favorite of yours, the *Ballos*. Stop thinking of Northern Greece and come and dance," she insists, pulling him to the floor.

One form of the *Ballos* dance is known as an "island" dance and is sometimes danced as a type of courtship ritual, with basic shuffling, promenade steps improvised by the couples. It is a gay, lively dance. On the dance floor, Yannis and Elena forget their differences. They enjoy each other, blend, complement each other's movements, respond to nuances, and become one with the music.

Yannis dances straight and tall, assertively wooing his partner. Elena plays her part well. She responds with coy, shy
movements and relishes assuming a submissive role as she
teases Yannis with her hips and arms while her eyes are
shyly lowered. Taking a scarf from her waist, she wraps it
around her hand and offers the other end to Yannis, so they
are joined by the kerchief and can dance without touching,
in the modest island fashion of couples who are courting.
On the dance floor, they are superb partners.

The *Ballos* ends, and the lead musician announces a
Zeibekiko is next. Arm resting protectively around Elena's
shoulder, Yannis asks again if they can talk as they walk to
the sofa.

"You want to talk?" Elena says. "But they are going to
play a *Zeibekiko*."

Yannis knows Elena will remain stubborn. He wants to
stop her taunting. "A *Zeibekiko*" Yannis says. "I will show
you a *Zeibekiko*."

And in deep frustration he moves away from Elena to the
dance floor, ready to perform the most famous of Greek
dances. It is a solo danced by men and is named after the
people of Zeybeks who lived in the hills near Smyrna when
it was burned to the ground in 1922. As danced by the sur-
vivors, the *Zeibekiko* expresses the pain of the refugees
forced to live in the hostile, urban ghettos of Athens.

Yannis' abilities as a dancer are known throughout
Mykonos, and other dancers gladly clear a space for him
when he appears on the floor. Even before the musicians
strike the first note, his posture and presence announce
that he has arrived. That he is there. That he is going
to dance.

Acknowledging Yannis' presence with nods, the musicians lift their instruments and Rhembetiko music fills the
Mykonos Bar. These songs of deep remorse for a lost

homeland began in the ghettos of Athens in the late 1920s, but some became integrated into modern Greek culture. They are popular on the islands and are enjoying a renewed popularity in Greece and America.

Under the dim lights, Yannis' body takes on the appearance of the music. His slender frame is wounded, darkened with torment. The ache in his heart escapes through his feet. He is at once one with the music and the musicians. With a glance toward him, the musicians embroider their playing to match his steps. At times, anticipating their musical wanderings, Yannis inspires them to increasingly creative and intricate passages.

His dancing is restrained, yet powerful; dramatic, yet introspective; precise, yet fluid. His execution of the *Zeibekiko* is his own, and he never dances it the same way twice.

The ghosts of the dancers from the hills of Smyrna and the ghettos of Athens join him, arm in arm, shoulder to shoulder, and when he circles the floor, their sorrow-bruised souls are with him. Yannis feels the presence of the other dancers first, and soon the audience feels it as well.

And then it begins. Ever so slowly. The first pink carnation is thrown and floats quietly to the floor. Next, white, red, and pink carnations are thrown and fall at Yannis' feet. Patrons scramble to buy bunches of flowers from the waiters to throw them at the dancer, as is the custom when Greeks are dancing. Soon everyone showers Yannis with flowers to show their admiration and appreciation until he is dancing on a bed of carnations.

Watching him, Elena feels longing. Memories flood through her and her face burns. When he dances, he is easy to love. His body is so expressive. His moves are so elegant. Her veins are pounding and she realizes it is to the rhythm of the music.

The musicians and Yannis pick up the tempo. As he moves deeper and deeper into himself, his dancing becomes more like an inward spiral. Moving counter-clockwise, his body expresses agitation, passion, frustration, and longing, but above all, pride. With each step, with each turn, his pride conquers the deep pain. It is this that holds the audience spellbound, the same quality imbedded in the Zeibekiko dancers and musicians of old, when there were no words to express their sorrow.

Elena knows he is dancing for her. She understands his torment. She suddenly feels off-center, as though she has lost the point of gravity in her body. Vertigo!

With a final flourish, the musicians end the song, and the people shout their delight and throw more flowers.

Breathless, Yannis stands still. His eyes are riveted on Elena's as he moves toward the door, motioning for her to follow him. She takes a cautious step forward, then pauses. Takes another step toward him, then spins backward and closes her eyes and lips tightly. As he stands outside waiting, Yannis does not hear her cry of pain as her teeth sink deep into her lower lip.

Yannis waits, resisting the urge to go back into the bar. When he realizes she is not following him, he resolves that this is his last effort to win her. "Tomorrow," he mutters as he walks away, "tomorrow I will sell more lobster and spaghetti than ever! More than ever!!

Arriving in Mykonos on the afternoon ferry, Matthew goes directly to his flat. Awaiting him is a note from Jim, saying he has finished his paper and will bring it to the next class. Jim says all is well; he and James are back safely, but had quite the adventure. Matthew smiles. He will talk to the boys soon; perhaps he will ask them to write a paper about their strange odyssey. First, he must find Elena.

As he walks slowly along the quay, he sees her almost immediately sitting at an outdoor taverna near "Mavro" Square where a bust of Manto Mavroyenous, the famous Greek heroine, sits proudly. Mavroyenous was an admiral in the Greek army during the 1821 uprising of the Greeks against Turkey and led troops, repulsing a Turkish invasion from the sea. She fought in a number of battles and gave all of her fortune to support the Greek war of independence. Sadly, she died in poverty on Paros in 1848.

Elena is painting a portrait of the five-year-old Nikos from his photograph. She has sketched a front-view portrait and is now framing his face with a mop of curly hair.

Upon seeing her, Matthew needs time to collect himself, so he stops to buy produce from the elderly women in native dress who have baskets of vegetables strapped to their donkeys. He is glad to be back in Greece and stops to survey the scene. Petros, the pink pelican and mascot of Mykonos, roams among the sea-side tavernas. Handsome men, tourists, stroll hand-in-hand along the boardwalk. Fashionably dressed visitors sit at small tables feasting on platters of *orektika*, various Greek appetizers. Fishermen sell red mullet and other delicacies arranged on large wooden tables near their boats. It appears that everything blends and flows together on the quay, a relatively small area where one can walk from one end to the other in less than ten minutes.

Matthew, seeing Elena, greets her warmly in Greek. "Πως εισαι;" (How are you?), he asks, and she responds, "Καλα ευχαριστω, και σεις;" (Fine, thank you. And you?)

He doesn't know why he is being so polite, but he is, and he asks if he may join her. She responds in Greek, "ναι, παρακαλω" (Yes, please), but when he sits beside her, she begins the conversation in English. She is very pleased to see him and smiles broadly. He is pleased as well. They grasp each other's hands. But both are trying to keep their true emotions in check.

They talk in an animated way. "It seems a year since I last saw you," Elena says. "We never did have a chance to talk much about your class. I enjoyed it so much. Please tell me more about what you are teaching."

"Good," he thinks, "this conversation will help me keep my composure." He then explains that he has been teaching lyric poetry for a number of years and especially enjoys the daily summer seminars on Delos. Elena says she knows something about the subject, but has forgotten much of the poetry she learned in high school. A bit defensively, Elena asks, "Why is it important in today's world, anyway?"

"It depends upon what appeals to you. Some people see beauty in a host of cavalry, others in a fleet of ships."

Elena laughs, but does not grasp the metaphor.

Matthew asks her whose portrait she is painting and she tells him, "My godson, Nikos."

"Besides my commissions, I make my living by selling paintings of scenes of Mykonos to tourists," she says. "But this painting is for me."

She says she admires what Matthew knows and teaches although history means little to her. Matthew answers saying that to his mind there is no history richer than that of Greece. "It is the very cradle of western civilization," he says.

Elena, her mind on other things, says: "Yes, our history is rich. But I have learned to live for the moment. I cannot envision the future, and my memories of the past are painful. Ah, but I don't want to be negative. Let me tell you what I enjoy. I enjoy dancing. Perhaps you would like to join me some evening? Greek dancing is very special. It's not disco dancing. I can't describe it. It has to be experienced."

"I don't dance, but I like to go for walks." He hesitates, then plunges ahead. "Perhaps we could go for another walk some evening? I enjoyed our last, uh, walk, before the winds came."

"Yes, I enjoyed it as well."

Matthew then begins to excuse himself, explaining he is teaching on Delos tomorrow. Also, he has a large number of pages from his current project to translate.

"Could I see you later tonight?" he asks.

"Let's talk about this later. Mykonos is such a small place. If I come to your place or you to mine, it will be all over town in an hour."

"I understand—forgive me for being pushy."

"You are not being pushy, it is just that our customs are strange here," she tries to explain, then, changing the subject, she asks, "Will you be teaching on ancient Delos or Big Delos?"

"I know of only one Delos," he exclaims with surprise.

"There is an island beyond the sacred place that is known to Mykoniates as 'Big Delos.' It appears on maps by another name, Rhenia."

Hearing the name, 'Rhenia,' Hera, the wife of Zeus, sits upright. "That is a long trip by sea," she muses, knowing that Sappho and Aphrodite have been searching for Poseidon. "Quickly, Hermes," she commands, "go and find Poseidon and do not come back until you locate him."

Dispatched by the fiery wife of the supreme god, the messenger leaves on winged sandals straight to the palace at the bottom of the sea. Sure enough, Poseidon lounges there on his throne, surrounded by nymphs and mermaids. An exhausted sea horse is by his side.

"Poseidon, where have you been?" Hermes asks. "I have been to this palace so many times; you were not here and the nymphs did not know your whereabouts."

"I was surveying my kingdom on my sea horse," Poseidon says. "I took my favorite mermaids with me."

"Come, Poseidon," Hermes implores. "Aphrodite and Sappho need your powers and Hera herself has sent me. Rise up from your throne and follow me!!"

"Rhenia," Matthew repeats. "Do people live there?"

"No. It is not allowed by the Greek government, and besides, there is no electricity and no fresh water. The island is primitive. There are a few concrete shelters, but that is all."

"A real primitive island?"

"Yes. Mykoniates take herds of sheep there by boat to graze, and men go there to fish and escape the tourists. I have been there, and it is surely the way Greece must have been in ancient times."

"It sounds beautiful."

"It's magic."

Matthew excitedly asks if he can take his class there, and she offers to be an escort and a guide.

Elena says, "I must attend an important town meeting tomorrow evening, but the following day I will be delighted to be your guide."

Sappho and Aphrodite are dancing with delight. Matthew and Elena are together again and Poseidon has been found!!

POSEIDON AND HERMES ON THEIR THRONES

The meeting to which Elena alluded concerns the volatile topic that has split the town in two—the expansion of the marina. Newspapers are published by the opposing sides and petitions circulated. Groups have been meeting separately to plan strategy, and town meetings are being held more frequently. Everyone is urged to attend. This particular meeting attracts many people, and, symbolically, Elena's parents are on one side of the room and Elena and her friends are again on the other. The talk goes on and on; Elena cannot wait until she can take Matthew to Rhenia.

ᛝᛝᛝ

That same evening, Matthew is in his flat and is summoned to answer the phone in the lobby. It is Claire, and she is breathless.

"Another problem has developed with the vote for the Senior Lectureship."

"Another problem?" Matthew queries. "What is it?"

"Our colleagues are very confused," Claire says.

"How could you tell?" Matthew asks.

"Is that meant as sarcasm? Oh, never mind, this is serious.

"I really must talk to you in person. I need a holiday anyway. Why don't I just come over there? I'll go to King's Row and bargain for a 'flight without villa.' There must be many charter cancellations at this time of year. I'll pack lightly, bring a swimming suit and sandals, and be there in a flash. Don't worry about anything. I'll leave Argos with friends. I'll see you soon, and we'll get everything sorted out straight away!"

"But, Claire," Matthew begins, but the blue-streaked comet is already on its way!

ᘓᘓᘓ

Disturbed by Claire's encroachment, Matthew decides on the following morning that he needs a diversion. He decides it is time to visit the Mykonos School for the Humanities and Dramatic Arts for Children where a friend of his, a scholar he first met at The British Library, is the Master of the school.

A man is standing outside the school and, as Matthew approaches, the man walks toward him, arms outstretched.

"Καλημερα, Καλημερα," the man says and calls Matthew "my good friend."

"Grigoris!" Matthew shouts. "Καλημερα, to you, my friend, how are you?"

Grigoris Petrides welcomes him warmly and tells him how delighted he is that he has finally visited the school.

"The children have gone home for the day," Grigoris explains, "but that is just as well for now we can talk."

"Ah, Grigoris, it is the children I want to hear about. What plans have you for their education?"

"As I told you when I accepted this position, we want to instill in our young boys and girls an appreciation of the history of Greece and of their Greek heritage."

"Do you do this through a study of the humanities?"

"Yes, through experiential study of the humanities and the performing arts. The next subject we will explore is 'Greece and the Sea.' I want them to learn important facts about our history, and then we will play and sing songs about the sea."

"Greece and the Sea," Matthew says. "Yes, your main link to the outside world is the sea. In ancient times it linked Greece with the great empires of the Middle East."

"As I recall, the entrepreneurs of the day founded colonies or city states in the west in Marseilles and Sicily and to the east in the Black Sea," Matthew continues.

"Correct," Grigoris replies, impressed, as always, by his friend's knowledge. "And the sea is still our main link. Until mid-century, there were many thriving little ports in Greece. It was really easier to travel by sea than by road."

Matthew makes the point that through the centuries Greek men made their living as fishermen. "Don't you have the largest merchant marine fleet in the world?" he asks, and Grigoris nods in the affirmative.

"Let me tell you how the sea affects our life today," Grigoris explains. "Because in Greece we are never more than a few hours' drive to the sea, this has made it easy for us to leave when times have been hard. And times have been hard many times in our recent history. Do you know that more than seven million Greeks now live overseas?"

"No, I did not know that. That's a significant loss."

"And that's all the more reason to teach these children all we can about Greece," the Master says emphatically, underscoring his reason for taking this position.

"I could not agree more. You are giving the children an excellent foundation upon which to build. You said you teach them the performing arts, as well. Tell me more about that."

"Well, we teach Greek dance, of course. All of our children must learn how to dance. To be Greek is to know how to dance. Or, to put it in the words of our great, world-renowned author Nikos Kazantzakis, 'to live is to dance, to dance is to live.'"

"The ancients talked about dance, too. What was Plato's famous comment?"

"Ah, 'a man who cannot dance is uneducated and unrefined!!'"

"Uneducated and unrefined?"

"Exactly. In his treatise on the education of the young, he placed great importance on exercise and dance. He said 'an accomplished dancer is the epitome of a cultured man.'"

"Yes, I suppose dance has always been uniquely important in your culture. I recall the many paintings of dancers on vases."

"It is an organic part of our culture. Do you recall the word 'ορχεσις,' which loosely translated is 'a single entity?'

"Yes, of course."

"Well, 'ορχεσις' was used by the ancients to describe just one movement, which included dance, music, and song. The word 'ορχεσις' makes no distinction between the three because they are a single entity."

"Fascinating. The children have a great master in you. You made the correct decision to leave the university and come here. It must be very rewarding."

"It is, it is. Can I interest you in a job here? One of my
instructors who teaches Classical Greek literature is leaving the island this summer for the mainland and I am in
need of a teacher. Can I interest you, Matthew?"

"Sounds tempting, but I may be promoted to a Senior
Lectureship at my university. Where is your instructor
going?"

"To Epidauros. He has a rare opportunity to produce
plays at that magnificent theatre."

"Indeed, and the acoustics!! It is the best-preserved
theatre. To think that it once seated 12,300 spectators. It's
a splendid treasure."

Grigoris beams at Matthew's comment and says, "This
glorious architectural treasure belongs to all of us."

Matthew says he would like to take his class to Athens
some summer and then visit the theatre at Epidauros. "If
the timing is right, would you do us the honor of accom-
panying us?"

"I would be honored," the Master says sincerely and
invites Matthew to visit again when the children will be
rehearsing.

As always, the men part with warm and sincere feelings.

As planned, on the third day of the seminar, Elena arranges for the class to travel on the *Chryso Pigi*, the boat used to take shepherds and their flocks to graze for the day on Big Delos. It is a large, sturdy boat that has made many trips from island to island. They leave in the late afternoon, because the sea was too choppy earlier.

"I must warn you that if a storm comes up there is no guarantee when we can return," Elena cautions Matthew. "Sometimes storms last for days and at other times they subside quickly, only to start up again the next day."

"I understand," says Matthew, remembering the fierce winds encountered by Odysseus!!

When they leave for Rhenia, he and his students are prepared to camp overnight. They have sleeping bags, food and water, lanterns, and other gear. They are prepared for adventure. As the boat rolls over the gentle waves nearing the island, Matthew tells the students they will examine, in detail, at least two more of Sappho's poems.

Brandon asks, "Do you think she was as good as Homer? Was she the female Home...?"

Jim breaks in immediately, "That question should not be asked."

James says quickly, "One should never compare Sappho to Homer, right, Professor?"

"That depends," Matthew says. "As students of the classics, you should all know that Sappho is a lyric poet, and Homer, on the other hand, composed the great epics."

Their attention is then focused on the beauty of the land they are approaching. When they arrive, the haunting solitude of the island mesmerizes Matthew and he is momentarily stunned. He and the class want to explore the island a bit before starting class, and Elena serves as a guide, leading them up a hill.

Patterns appear in semicircles from the top of the hill to the lower ground, and upon closer inspection it becomes clear the arrangements are stone fences. Elena explains the fences are to keep grazing animals confined to certain areas. It is a practice, she explains, that is done today, just as it must have occurred in ancient times.

"We don't know how old these stone fences are," she says. "People of all ages use what they have to build shelters and dividers, and the stones have always been here and on other islands."

They follow the fences past small, white, concrete homes scattered about that provide temporary shelter to shepherds. Most likely they are walking over ancient graves, but if there were once markers, they have long since disappeared.

When they reach the top they turn to the sea. It languishes before them, undisturbed and silent, except for the gentle lapping of waves. The island is so still they can hear themselves breathe. The sea is tinted deepening shades of blue, green, and purple. Near the shore the color is a subtle blue, becoming a bright blue/green and then a rich, dark, wine-colored purple in its deepest part. Matthew, Elena, and the students look toward the cove through which the boat passed to reach this island.

Mighty pillars, crowned by clouds, guard the entrance to this primitive paradise. On one side, the huge rocks are rugged and weather-beaten, their age hidden in the dark stones. On the other side, the surfaces are so smooth and shiny, reflecting the rays of the sun, that the giant stones appear newly risen from a protective cave in the sea. Proud as sentries these pillars stand, ancient companions to the sea.

Breaking the spell, Elena suggests gently that it is time to begin the class. Following the stone fence, they reach the beach and assemble under a rickety wooden shelter that has the remains of a bonfire nearby.

Elena leaves the class, saying she plans to sketch. She is feeling content and peaceful, and she plans to practice her asanas as well.

Matthew begins his lecture: "On the boat ride over here, I explained to James that, while Homer wrote in epic form, the poems of Sappho are lyrics. Can someone tell me the origin of the term 'lyric poem'?"

"The word lyric is from lyre, the musical instrument," Kallirroi says.

"Correct, and how is the lyre connected with Sappho?"

"I read that her poetry was intended to be accompanied by music," Christos offers.

"Yes, and in ancient times, that instrument usually was...?"

"The lyre, of course," Christos answers.

"Now Sappho did not tell us directly that her songs were to be sung to the accompaniment of the lyre, did she?"

"No," Brandon says, "but there is evidence."

"Such as?"

James says, "In one poem she says, 'Come divine lyre, speak to me and find yourself a voice.'"

"Very good."

"In another," Brandon continues, "she says, 'And I shall now sing these songs beautifully to delight my companions.'"

"Sappho's contemporary, Alcaeus, mentions the lyre at a banquet," Jim says.

"And in another poem he uses the verb, ψαλλω, meaning 'I pluck the lyre strings,'" James contributes.

"Excellent. Can anyone cite any other evidence?"

"The vase painters," Brandon offers. "When I see Sappho depicted on vases, it is with a lyre."

"Bravo, bravo," Matthew praises the class, "and there is other evidence as well. For example, when Horace refers to Sappho and Alcaeus, he mentions their lyres. Can you imagine how wonderful it must have been to listen to beautiful words sung to a stringed instrument? Without amplified sound? You could actually hear the words!! Imagine!!"

Matthew continues, "So that you can better understand what makes lyric poetry unique, I have a special assignment on the meter in which Sappho's poetry was written that I

will explain at the end of the class, but for now, let's concentrate on the homework I gave. I asked you to take the
fragment commonly referred to as 'Sappho's Apple'
and translate the sense of this into modern English. Any
volunteers?"

Elena, who is sketching nearby, is listening. Dina volunteers and reads her translation:

> You are to me a lone red apple,
> high atop the tallest tree.
> Some say all who came
> passed it by; I say none
> could reach that high.

"That is lovely, Dina, but how do you get the word 'lone'
from the Greek word 'γλυκυμαλον' Matthew asks. "The
root of that word is 'γλυκυ,' meaning 'sweet.'"

"Yes, I know," Dina responds, "but most apples are
sweet. This apple is unique, so I called it 'lone.'"

"Very interesting and very nice. Bravo.

"Let's continue the examination," Matthew says. "Why is
it none could reach that high?"

Some students say the apple represents perfection, others say unattainable desire.

"What else could the apple represent?" Matthew asks as
he prods the students to think more deeply about this
image. They answer:

"A high ideal."

"A solitary person."

"Someone elusive."

"A temptation."

"Someone who is untouched, is pure."

"And what is one name for someone who is untouched
or pure?" Matthew asks.

"A virgin?" a student asks.

"Yes," Matthew says, "that is a possibility."

"What does the apple mean, then?" asks Brandon. "What did Sappho intend? Is it a high ideal, someone unattainable? A temptation? A solitary person, or a virgin?"

Dina asks, "Yes, what did Sappho intend?"

"I think whatever you see in the apple is what Sappho intended," Matthew responds. "Think more about this image," he encourages, "and we will discuss it further."

"Before our next class," Matthew continues, "I want you to read the chapters on Sapphic meters, sometimes called stropes. The use of these meters enabled Sappho to express in a very sincere and delicate way the depth of her feelings. Her words flow effortlessly, gracefully, and melodiously. The secret of her excellence can be found in these meters. I will bring a chalkboard for the next class and demonstrate.

"Gilbert Highet, the great classical scholar, believes these meters were developed from Greek song and dance rhythms, which he describes as subtle and complex. It's a fascinating theory."

The class is over; the students walk along the beach to explore the island. Elena is on the far side, engrossed in her practice, but Matthew is now standing quietly and watching her. As she stretches, her fingers seem to touch the sky, and her body, clothed in white, becomes a sculpture that is one with the island.

"So that is poetry in motion," Matthew muses.

Suddenly, a storm materializes.

Loukas, the fisherman from the *Chryso Pigi*, runs to Elena. "You must decide at once to leave immediately or stay the night," Loukas declares. "A bad storm is developing."

"Would we be safe if we returned now?" Matthew asks.

"There are no guarantees," Elena says. "I think it is safer to stay the night."

"I agree," concurs Loukas. "It could rapidly become a 10 Beaufort wind."

"What does that mean?" asks Matthew.

"At a 10 on the Beaufort scale, the winds will become a whole gale and travel at 55 to 63 miles an hour," the fisherman explains.

Matthew cannot take chances with the students' lives. Gathering the students around him, he instructs them to disperse to the shelters for cover and to remain there until the storm dies down.

"Men in one shelter and women in the other," he orders.

"Yeh, right," the students say.

"Elena," the fisherman says, "there are men nearby who came here in a small, private boat to fish. I will take you and your friend to them and you can stay there."

Loukas introduces Matthew and Elena. "These are my friends, Angelos and Phillipos, and they will give you shelter for the night."

Angelos and Phillipos urge them to spend the night on board. The quarters are close, and Matthew and Elena share a small space where their bodies constantly touch, especially as the wind rocks the caique. It is just the excuse they need to curl up in a close embrace and share some tender kisses and caresses. The night, with its howling winds and thunderbolts thrown by the gods, becomes almost mystical. For more than an hour there appears to be a magic show in the heavens as the sky is punctuated with brilliant flashes of light.

Abruptly, the storm subsides.

"Never have I seen a storm of such force end so swiftly—I swear by all the gods—and never has the sky been so bright," the first fisherman, Angelos, says.

"In all my years—St. Nikolaos is my witness—I have never felt such force," Phillipos, the second fisherman declares.

"It is safe now for you two to leave the boat, but stay close by—I implore you—because this is a strange night," Angelos says.

Within minutes after calm prevails, it becomes possible for Matthew and Elena to leave the boat for a period and walk on the island where moonlight is tentatively breaking through grey clouds, but they remain close to the boat.

The stars are barely visible, but one star in particular is noticeable because it is shining and seems to be always directly above them.

As they experience the island's haunting beauty and magic, they walk hand-in-hand. Matthew says to Elena, "I saw you do your yoga routine, you know—I could not help but see you."

"It is not called a routine. I call it 'doing my *asanas*,'" Elena corrects him.

"Ah, your asanas. Well, your asanas are quite impressive indeed. How can you bend your body into those postures? I could not begin to touch my forehead to my knees."

"But you could, you could. Your body will do it. It is your mind that is holding you back. All you have to do is let go," she explains.

"Are you telling me that it is mind over matter?" Matthew asks.

"Yes, Matthew, you could do it. You could touch your forehead to your knees. All you have to do is let go."

At this pronouncement, Matthew lets go of Elena's hand. Deliberately, he places his arm around her waist and pulls her closer to him as they continue walking. "I missed you," Matthew says.

"When you were gone, my heart hurt," she responds.

They sit under the moonlight, wondering if they could remain on the beach overnight, but remembering the fisherman's warning, they return to the boat.

The fishermen, lanterns in their hands, are standing beside the boat.

"We are going to sleep nearby on the beach," Angelos says. "We have lanterns for light and we have blankets. There are extra blankets on board for you."

"There is plenty of room for both of you to sleep and you will be comfortable," Phillipos graciously offers.

Matthew and Elena board the boat and the fishermen are nearby on the beach. Soon they see Matthew raising his hands over his head and bending, almost as if he is bowing to someone. Then they see Elena raising her hands high above her head and disappearing from their sight as she bows, and raising her hands high above her head again. They see Matthew standing, watching Elena, as she bends and sways her body into various postures. It appears that Matthew is trying to imitate her movements.

Hearing their laughter, Angelos asks his companion, "Phillipos, you have more experience in the ways of the world than I have—is that a new dance?"

"Who knows?" Phillipos responds. "Maybe they are showing respect to the gods so we can all return tomorrow."

Angelos says, "Maybe they are invoking the gods so that we never return!!"

Finally exhausted from the day's excitement, Matthew and Elena wrap themselves in blankets for warmth and make themselves comfortable on the small bunk, resisting the overwhelming impulse for total intimacy. The fishermen are too near. So they steal kisses and stroke each other and talk until they are sleepy, and then sleep fitfully until dawn.

Before everyone else awakens, the students are up and about, swimming in the cool waters. Last night they ignored Matthew's instructions of "men in one shelter and women in another" and separated according to their inclinations. Brandon and Kallirroi slept in one, Dina and Christos in another, and James and Jim were in the third. What happened in these shelters is nobody's business.

After the magic night, it is almost with reluctance that Matthew, Elena, and their new friends, Angelos and Phillipos, gather the students and leave on a calm sea for Mykonos.

James and Jim tell Matthew they would like to visit Santorini. He readily agrees with their choice, saying it is one of the most beautiful of all the islands.

"We want to visit the site of the Lost Continent of Atlantis," James explains.

"You understand, of course," Matthew says, "that Atlantis is a myth, a legend, first told by the Greek ruler Solon in 590 B.C. and then embellished by Plato in 370 B.C."

"What is the legend of Atlantis?" Jim asks.

Matthew explains, "Plato tells us the gods destroyed Atlantis because its leaders were filled with pride and its people complacent. In one day and night, according to Plato, the gods flooded the continent of Atlantis and it sank into the sea, never to be found again."

"Isn't there a dormant volcano on Santorini?" James asks.

"Yes, the island is famous for that. Archaeologists believe there was an apocalyptic catastrophe on the island around 1450 or 1500 B.C. that dramatically altered the history of the ancient world. They believe giant tidal waves roared toward Crete, destroying the Minoan civilization there and the Palace of Knossos."

"Is the volcano still there?"

"You will see."

"We must see Santorini—thanks for all the information."

"Be careful and try not to have another misadventure. And remember, there is another paper due."

"I've almost finished my paper," James says. "i'm taking it with me to revise it."

"Do you think that's a good idea?" Matthew asks. "Remember what you said happened before."

"It did happen, but I suppose you will continue to doubt us."

"Indubitably," Matthew says.

ᑕᑐᑕᑐᑕᑐ

In town, Elena's parents, her brother, and little Nikos are by the wharf, buying fish from the fishermen when Elena suddenly appears. Her parents are soon joined by Elena's grandparents and several aunts. A religious holiday is approaching, and the family is obviously shopping together.

Elena is delighted to see her loved ones, and she embraces all and greets them in her native tongue.

"Πως εισαι, πως εισαι;" (How are you? How are you?)

Her grandparents and aunts reply in Greek.

"Καλα, Ελενη, και συ;" (Fine, Elena, and you?)

Her mother calls her Helen, but Elena ignores this and continues to talk in Greek, as does her family. Elena asks, "How is everyone and how is Nikos?"

The women, now grouped together a bit awkwardly, shoulder-to-shoulder with Elena's parents, reply in unison:

"We are fine, Helen, we are fine."

"Come home, Helen, come home."

Elena does not know how to respond. She tells her black-shawled relatives she must leave and then shrieks, "I love you, but why can't you love me for who I am?"

Her mother responds: "Helen, do you know who you are? Do you know who you are?"

Elena hurries away and walks to the end of the quay, approaching one of the 350 churches on the island. Most of these churches are attached to private homes, and it is a status symbol to have a chapel on private property, but this place of worship is for the community.

A wedding is about to take place, and the wedding party is approaching. They are dressed in traditional Greek wedding garments and will be married by one of the oldest priests on the island. The priest has a long beard that once was black but now is snow white, peppered with just a hint of grey. He is dressed in long black robes and a tall black *klimafi*, crowns his head. One of Elena's friends, about to enter the church to see this unique and beautiful ceremony, invites Elena to join her. She declines and hurries off.

ᓚᓚᓚ

As the ferry approaches Santorini, James and Jim are awestruck. The island looks mysterious, other-worldly, with clouds floating in a semicircle above a crescent-shaped, lava-colored cliff. As the boat approaches, they see a gigantic cliff whose ancient rocks of red, black, brown, and grey have not shed the lava bath. The cliff is more than 300 meters high and goes straight up. They realize that they are approaching what was the belly of the volcano. White houses, resembling tiny boxes, are arranged around the rim of this vast apocalyptic wonder. The town is on the volcano's rim with the caldera, or crater, below.

They are in Fira, the island's capital, and intend to ride donkeys up the narrow pathway that zigzags 260 meters above the sea. They have been told the views are breath-taking.

As they stroll toward the crowd waiting to ride the beasts, Jim asks James what topic he has chosen for their next paper.

"I have written an essay that is sort of historical—it examines Sappho's place in history as one of the greatest poetesses of all time."

Alas, there is a rumbling high above, and the once complacent clouds, hovering quietly over the volcano's rim, are now shaking. Sappho is in a rage. "Did you hear that, my sister?" Sappho asks Aphrodite. "He called me a poetess. A poetess!! A poet is a poet is a poet is a poet. I am a poet. I am not a poetess."

"Sappho, Sappho," Aphrodite says, "the poor uninformed mortal made a mistake. At least he said you are one of the greatest in all of history!!"

"He will pay for this insult," Sappho warns, sending Hermes to find his son, the lesser god Pan.

James and Jim prepare to mount the donkeys, and old men who are the caretakers of the beasts help them.

"What is the name of this donkey?" James asks.

"Sisyphus," the guide says. "All the donkeys are named Sisyphus."

"Why?"

The guide, who must have told the story a thousand times, begins: "Sisyphus was the King of Corinth. One day he saw an eagle carry away a fair maiden and he suspected this was done by the will of Zeus. He reported the abduction to the girl's father in exchange for a supply of water for the citadel in Corinth, thus incurring Zeus' wrath. As punishment, Zeus condemned Sisyphus to eternally roll a rock to the top of the hill. Before the rock reached the top, it would fall down and Sisyphus had to roll it up again."

"So the donkeys just keep going up and down the hill?"

"Up and down, up and down."

"Don't they protest?"

"They are impassive. Sometimes we have to check to make sure they are breathing."

"Well," Jim says. "It sure looks like a steep climb to me. I want to leave my backpack here. I don't want anything to fall out while I'm riding up there."

"Here," James says, handing him the paper he has written on Sappho, "please put my paper in your backpack for safekeeping."

"Pan," Sappho orders, "leave the nymphs alone for now, stop all your merriment, and listen to what I have summoned you to do. Please be serious."

"Thank you for summoning me, sister with the golden throat," Pan sings. "You have chosen a wild place for your mischief and I adore wild places."

Sappho whispers into his ear. "You want me to take the form of what?" Pan asks. "I would rather be a goat. Why can't I be a goat?"

"Not a goat, Pan. Do this one favor for me and I will write an ode especially for you."

"Your words are as melodic as my music," Pan says. "I will do this for you, mellifluous one."

As James hands his paper to Jim, the donkey becomes greatly agitated. His owner, Elias, has never seen him like this. Elias shrieks and moves quickly away to escape his kicks. With one swift motion, the donkey, still kicking, turns and bites James on the backside. James yelps and turns as the donkey starts to take a second bite, but this time the beast bites the paper James is holding in his right hand. The donkey proceeds to eat the composition, making sure he chews every single page!

Screaming and ranting in Greek, Yannis, the man tending the donkey, shouts and gestures at the animal and the boys. A crowd has now gathered. Yannis walks slowly around the beast, examining him, shaking his head, gesturing and speaking rapidly.

"Oh, no," Jim says, "the donkey ate the paper!! Do you have another copy?"

"No, no. I can't believe this has happened. Neither will Dr. Wyttman. He'll never believe us."

SAPPHO   JAMES   SISYPHUS   ELIAS   PAN   JANNIS   TOURIST

As Matthew returns to his flat, the manager calls to him, saying there is again a telephone message from the students. He hands him a slip of paper.

"I took the message as best I could," the manager says, "but I could not understand everything the boys were saying because they were speaking from a cellular phone and there were men in the background screaming curses. I have not heard such curses in many a year."

"Really," Matthew says.

"The message is that they are on their way back to Mykonos, but James needs time to write another paper. A donkey named Sisyphus bit James and then ate his paper."

"A donkey bit Sisyphus?"

"No, a donkey named Sisyphus bit your student."

"Let me see that message," Matthew says, taking the paper. "This says a donkey bit Jim and then ate James' paper."

"I wrote that incorrectly," the manager says. "The donkey bit James, not Jim, and then ate James' paper."

"But the donkey ate the paper?"

"Yes, that is correct."

"That is asinine, asinine," Matthew says.

"What did you say?" the manager asks.

"Asinine," Matthew emphasizes.

リリリ

Matthew goes to his flat to sort out this latest news. He'll talk to James and Jim when they return, but for now, he needs time to himself. Matthew relaxes with his afternoon tea and enjoys his solitude. Standing near his window, he begins to stretch and raises his arms high above his head. Slowly, he bends and tries to touch his forehead to his knees. Concentrating and remembering Elena's words, he tries several times, but cannot complete the bend.

"Elena makes it look so easy," Matthew says with admiration.

Just a few sessions remain as the seminar is now coming to a close. Because of the storm, Matthew decides to direct the remaining classes on sacred Delos, nearer to Mykonos than "Big Delos." He is grateful, however, that he had experienced the magic island. Elena is now part of the group and the students have accepted her as Matthew's girlfriend. She tells Matthew she wants to complete renderings of the lions who once guarded the Sacred Lake. Also, she says, "I want to be with you." Her physical desire for him is keen, but he is also becoming an indispensable, calm refuge.

The students seem anxious for the seminar to end. Brandon and Kallirroi find excuses to be together, reading poetry to each other, and Dina and Christos are more absorbed in each other than in the class. Matthew is finding it difficult to keep their attention focused on the subject matter. James and Jim, who returned last night, are most attentive, have turned in all their papers, and continuously praise Sappho's poetry. They did not object when Matthew asked each to write a paper on "your strange odyssey," as he called their adventures.

Sensing the general inattention, however, Matthew hurries through the lecture and does not ask for much participation. When the class is over, Elena approaches him. The students watch, giggle, and begin to disperse. Matthew asks if they plan to go to the gift shop or return to Mykonos, and when they say they are heading for the boat, he says he will see them tomorrow then for one last time.

Elena shows him her watercolors and they walk and talk together, walking farther from the group. They walk toward Mt. Kynthos, the highest point of the island.

"The remains of two temples are on the mountain," Elena explains, pointing. "One is for the goddess Athena Kynthia and the other is dedicated to the god Zeus Kynthios."

"What other treasurers does this mountain hold?" Matthew asks.

"Farther down are a cave-temple dedicated to Hercules; a temple to Zeus' wife Hera, one of the oldest temples on the site; and a sanctuary for the Egyptian gods, Isis, Sarapis, Osiris, and of the Syrian gods Adad and Atargati. The Isis Temple is the best preserved and offers a perfect view of the entire island."

"For one who claims to have little interest in history, you certainly are well-informed," Matthew comments with pleasure.

"I've been here many times; for me this is not history."

"This is spectacularly steep," Matthew says as they come to the foot of the mountain.

"Yes, but those who climb to the top are rewarded with outstanding views of all of Delos, plus nearby islands, including the island of Syros. Have you ever climbed Mt. Kynthos?" Elena asks.

"No," he responds, and accepts her unspoken challenge by walking with her toward the steps leading to the top.

It is an arduous climb up narrow, steep, and slippery steps. One cannot ascend casually, but must maneuver to get the best footing. Matthew is glad he wore a thin shirt and shorts. Elena is also dressed in light clothing and has fastened her long hair to the top of her head with a barrette. She carries a small basket containing the lunch she packed.

When they get to the top they rest. They are thrilled by the view. Matthew sees poetry, and Elena sees forms and colors. Matthew's eyes travel over the islands circling Delos and he suddenly says to Elena:

"This island to the left of us. Is it Rhenia, the one we were on?"

"Yes, that is Rhenia, my magic island."

"It is magic, Elena. It is hauntingly beautiful. It would be haunting even without the ancient burial grounds."

After a while it is déjà vu. A storm begins to develop and the wind swirls around them. It is eerie. The sky is still bright, but the force of the winds is a good indication that a serious storm is about to begin. "Ah, my purple-cloaked sister," Sappho sings, "it was worth waiting for Poseidon!!" "Yes, silver-tongued maiden, it was," Aphrodite agrees.

"Matthew, the cave I told you about is nearby. We must find it," Elena shouts above the wind.

"Here it is, over here. Hurry, come in."

They take shelter in the ancient cave and, as they enter, there is still enough light for them to see inside. There are remnants of a number of small fires, a small pile of unused kindling wood, blankets, empty cans and bottles, and the remains of picnic lunches. Other people have found refuge here.

They gather sticks of kindling wood for a fire. Using bunches of twigs as lanterns to guide them in the dark, they go a bit deeper into the cave and build a small fire there.

After several tries, they light the kindling, gather enough wood to keep it going, and then relax. The storm begins in earnest and they realize they have missed the last boat to Mykonos; they are stranded for the night. Neither is frightened. Each is a bit bemused by the experience.

"What do you think, Elena, is this a situation where if you've seen one cave you've seen them all?"

"I think not. This is a sacred, prehistoric cave."

"Is it, indeed? You are sure no vendors will appear to sell us souvenirs," Matthew teases.

"Not in this storm; no vendors will appear. For your information, Professor Wyttman, this is the cave where legend says Hercules was worshiped."

"This very cave?"

"Yes, at least this is what the tour guides told me."

"We are quite special then to be chosen by the gods to be stranded here."

Laughing, Elena says, "We are either chosen by gods or very foolish adventurers!!"

In Elena's basket are a blanket, a picnic lunch, and a jug of wine. She spreads the blanket on the cave floor and offers Matthew fruit, yogurt, and a spinach pie. She opens the jug of wine and they drink, sharing the single cup she brought.

The storm subsides as quickly as it began.

The mountaintop is bathed in moonlight and light from the stars. Through the cave's entrance they see the golden rays from a single star that appears to rival the moon in size.

Matthew and Elena both know the night will be long, and each is a bit awkward. Taking control, Matthew decides to set a comfortable tone for now.

"Tell me about your family," Matthew asks, knowing that there are problems.

"Ah, my family—there are many things that cannot be spoken."

Matthew encourages her to talk and tell him about her life. He wants to learn what is troubling this lovely woman. His desire is mounting. He wants to know everything about her.

"You live near your family, don't you?" he asks.

She hesitates, then says, "I live very near them."

"You know I rent a flat at the Nissaki," Matthew says. "It's very comfortable with great views."

"I was born there," Elena says.

"At the Nissaki?" Matthew asks in wonderment.

"No, I was born in a home on the beach where the hotels are now. My parents lived in a big home and my grandparents lived in a smaller home next door. My aunts and uncles lived nearby. That property was in our family for generations. We owned the land; that is where I lived my childhood."

"What happened?"

"I can't describe it."

"Elena…"

"The holidays were the best, especially the Feast of the Trinity, fifty days after Easter."

Elena then describes the wonderful day before the actual feast day when the family cooked at her grandparents' house.

"Huge spits were mounted above open fires. Whole lambs sprinkled with fresh rosemary slowly roasted for hours. My mother and my aunts baked round loaves of wheat bread and pastries and baklava for days before the holiday. They brought baskets of the loafs, along with their Greek food specialties, to the feast. I remember the long tables where all of us would sit, passing platters of eggplant, moussaka, tomatoes, and grilled fish fresh from the sea. We began our meal in the late afternoon, first with a fish course, then the lamb, followed by other fish courses. We drank wine made by my grandfather and aged in a cellar he designed. Platters of eggplant and okra in tomato sauce were passed, along with plates of plain cucumbers and kalamata olives sprinkled with olive oil and mint. We ate slowly, savoring every morsel. Long after sunset we were still eating the pastries and other desserts."

"How beautiful," Matthew says.

"The day after this treat was very spiritual," Elena says. "All of us, my parents, grandparents, aunts and uncles, my brother, nieces and nephews, went in two large boats to Rhenia for the religious celebration of the Feast of the Trinity led by the Greek Orthodox priests. We were just one large family among the many boatloads of Greeks who came each year from Mykonos and Tinos to Rhenia to celebrate this holy day.

"Those are my childhood memories."

"Elena, what happened?"

Taking a deep breath, Elena proceeds to explain. "The town leaders and men called 'developers' tricked my family."

"How did they trick them?"

"They told them about the wonderful future that is possible for everyone on Mykonos, especially the young people, if they would only sell our land for progress.

"The politicians first convinced people who owned land on the beach to allow a road to be built down to their homes. Next, plans were presented for a development scheme 'for the future of Mykonos.' Tempting amounts of money were offered for the properties, and my parents and other relatives agreed to sell all the land."

"Where are they now?"

"They are scattered throughout the island. My parents live near me, near the windmills, but the rest of my family is scattered about.

"They destroyed my childhood memories.

"How can I tell you how precious it was to always anticipate the scents of lilac and roses from tiny, perfumed cushions in a bureau drawer, to feel the wood of my grandmother's table, or to see my relatives cooking and eating together? I cannot bear to think about it, and I cannot imagine how I could rear a child any differently than I was reared," Elena laments. "I cannot talk about this anymore."

Close to tears, Elena says, "Pain falls, drop by drop, upon my heart."

"Elena," Matthew begins.

But Elena interrupts him by declaring, "I miss living day by day with my parents, and I especially miss my godson, Nikos."

Elena has a need to continue talking, and it is as though the words now flow from her. Matthew encourages her, hoping that as she talks, healing will begin.

"My family believes I am denying who I am, but they do not understand how important my past is to my identity," she laments. "When my parents talk about their love of Greece, they mean they love our history and all things that make us Greeks, especially our religion; to me this land means my memories, too.

"My parents did not understand it at the time, and they were naive and tricked by the developers. They took money in exchange for the precious remembrances from my childhood. Now the developers want to trick them again. It was so painful for me when they sold our land before, I will do everything I can to prevent the developers from winning again. Now they want to destroy the windmills, our historic landmarks. I spent so much of my childhood near those windmills. That is where my grandfather began to tell me the stories of our great poet Homer and the amazing campaigns of Alexander the Great.

"I am fighting the developers because if they tear down those windmills, they will destroy the last remembrances of my childhood. Everything will then be taken away from me. I will no longer know who I am."

Matthew holds her close to him to comfort her.

"Elena, in my opinion, you are unique in the way you express who you are. When you perform your graceful yoga, you are saluting Greece!!"

"Really, Matthew."

"Really. And through your watercolors, you capture these lovely islands with colors that cannot be expressed with words.

"I wish I could be more expressive myself," he continues. "Through knowing

you, I am just now beginning to realize that I most often express myself by teaching the words of others."

Elena touches Matthew's face and slowly moves her fingers from his forehead to his lips. She pauses, resting her fingertips gently on his lips. Turning to face her, Matthew starts to caress her hair, but the large barrette holds her silken strands firmly in place. He pulls her closer to him and holds her protectively, encouraging her to talk about her plans for the future. He tries to delay embracing her, for he knows once he starts he will not want to stop.

"The past is fading and I cannot envisage the future, especially with Yannis. My dreams do not match his."

"Is Yannis the man who was waiting for you by the boat? Does he want to share your life, to live with you?"

"Yes, he is a good person, hard-working. He wants to live a simple life, away from the tourists. He dreams of αυταρκεια. He wants to be independent. His dream is to be self-sufficient, to live on a farm, and maybe have his own leather business. I cannot imagine life in a small village.

"What are your dreams, Matthew?"

"I straddle two worlds," he says evasively, and removing his arm from around Elena, he adjusts his posture, placing both arms around his knees. Elena sits upright as well. "One world is very safe, very predictable."

"And the other world?"

"The other world is fraught with danger. Danger from an Aegean goddess with deep, dark eyes. But it is also very exciting."

"We are becoming too philosophical," proclaims Elena, blushing. "Entertain me now. Recite some poetry."

She asks Matthew to recite some verses she remembers studying and he says only if she will, as well.

Sappho is playing her lyre and does not hear Elena's suggestion about reciting poetry. Aphrodite does not want her to become offended if the recitations are not to her liking, so she urges Sappho to go to the next cloud and take a nap. Stifling a yawn, the poet agrees.

Matthew recites, first in the beautiful language of ancient Greece, and then in his native English. She is enchanted, and recites a few poems she remembers as well.

Golden light from a single star and a full moon shines over this most sacred of islands. Inside the cave, the light of the fire bathes Matthew and Elena in an amber glow. He is now lying on the blanket with Elena relaxing next to him, gazing into his eyes, admiring how soft, warm, and peaceful they are.

Suddenly, a strong breeze whirls around Matthew and Elena, and there is a brilliant flash. For a moment it seems as though there is another presence in the cave.

By now, the poetry has worked its charms on Elena. It has entered her soul; she is overcome with a powerful emotion. Filled with desire, Elena decides to act. She leans over Matthew, takes the barrette from her hair, and with one deft flourish, brushes her long, silken strands up and down the length of him. The suddenness of her movements and the sensation of silken hair brushing his body is thrilling. Slowly and tenderly, she continues to brush his body with her hair. He gasps with surprise and excitement, and chills cover him. Then she kisses him, long and deep, and slowly. She opens his shirt and brushes him again, ever so lightly, with her chiffon strands. Matthew has never, ever felt a similar sensation. And he has never, ever been kissed like that.

Before he can take any initiatives, she uses her yoga skills. She positions her arms on either side of him, lifts herself up and balances herself above him for a few seconds. Then, in a slow, dream-like motion, she lowers her body over his. She responds to directions indicated by his touches, stretching her legs far to each side, arching her back high and pressing her body firmly over his, at once opening herself to him, but covering him possessively. He unbuttons her shorts, removes her top, and slowly traces the outlines of her small breasts with just the tips of his moist fingers. His fingertips make feather-like traces over the outline of her lips, then back to her breasts, sending shivers through her. He stares into her eyes, caressing her methodically, almost dispassionately. This is enormously exciting to Elena, who is unaccustomed to such studied lovemaking.

Pulling her toward him, his lips dust her delicate breasts as he cups first one, then the other, tracing their contours now with just the apex of his tongue. Elena moves over him slowly, back and forth, offering herself, challenging him to take her. Matthew suddenly becomes still. He fixes his eyes intently upon her, penetrating her with his gaze. Deliberately, he stretches his hands over his head, keeping his eyes locked with hers. His stillness forces her to break the spell, to act, to follow her desires. Moaning softly, she stretches her body over his, covers his mouth with hers, and guides his proud manhood into her welcoming temple.

The lovers mate; the gods rejoice. And Aphrodite blushes.

The next morning, they are up before dawn in order to avoid being seen, and descend the mountain, hand-in-hand. Playfully, they hide behind the Temple of Isis and wait until the souvenir shop opens and the first tour group arrives. They will return to Mykonos with that group on the next boat. When the doors open, they are the first inside and relax over coffee and cheese pies.

Matthew wanders through the shop, looking for presents for Elena. He selects two reproductions with details of mosaic floors, one from the House of Trident, with the famous drawing of the Dolphin and the anchor, and the second from the House of Dolphins, showing Eros-Hermes leading two dolphins. On the other side of the shop, Elena is shopping as well for a gift for Matthew. She buys a reproduction of the marble lions guarding the Sacred Lake.

Outside, some visitors surround the tour guide and others wander about. Matthew and Elena use this opportunity to gradually blend in with the group, first admiring the mosaics and then some of the island's most famous sculptures. "Come this way," Elena calls to Matthew. He follows her to ruins of the Precinct of Dionysus with its famous altar of abundantly proportioned phallic symbols.

"What do you think of this?" she asks, pointing to the remains of a whimsical sculpture of a huge penis.

"I'm envious."

"You shouldn't be."

The group comes their way and they blend in, telling the guide they have lost their tags. He is unconcerned and motions for them to follow along.

The guide asks the tourists questions, such as, "Who can tell me what was stored in this temple?"

No one answers and Elena nudges Matthew. He asks, "Trophies from battles?"

"Why, yes," the guide says. "Now, can someone tell me what mosaic is in this temple?"

Matthew nudges Elena and she asks, "Is it the mosaic of Dionysus on a panther that is Delos' best known treasure?"

The guide is surprised, and Matthew and Elena then leave the group to take the first boat back to Mykonos. While Elena is affectionate and stays close to Matthew, he becomes uncomfortable and retiring while still polite and thoughtful. He is enormously confused. At times he feels frightened. His emotions are on a rollercoaster, and he is rapidly losing control. There are so many things happening in his relationship with Elena that are unpredictable, out of his control. This is a new experience for him; he feels exposed, vulnerable. How should he relate to this enchanting creature who has disturbed his world? What does she mean to his life?

When the boat docks, he says, "I'm sorry, Elena, but I
must be alone now to prepare for my final seminars." He
hesitates and says, "I will be in touch," then departs without saying when they will meet again. Elena is now confused. Her heart hurts.

Later that afternoon, Elena sees that Matthew is teaching
his final class by the quay (he could not handle the emotions of going back to Delos), and she thinks this is
strange. He did not expect to see Elena at the quay. She
lingers until class is over; he feels awkward and perplexed.

"Matthew, would you like to go dancing at the Mykonos
Bar? Even if you don't want to dance, you can enjoy the
atmosphere and see traditional Greek dances. It is much
fun and very lively."

Matthew almost accepts, but then declines, mentioning
his need to complete his translations. But he is of two
minds. He explains that his students are leaving the island
tomorrow and he wants to say goodbye to them now.

"Tomorrow morning it will be very crowded at the harbor. It will be nicer to say our goodbyes here," Matthew
tells Elena. He does not invite her to join them, and once
again she is deeply hurt. Awkwardly, he leaves her and
walks toward the students, turning his full attention to
them.

Some of them are going island-hopping and others are
returning to Athens. They seem to have matured during the
summer, and he is proud of their progress as students and
of their resourcefulness. The pleasure of teaching them and
the beauty of the islands would make this experience a special part of his memories.

Embracing each individually, Matthew wishes them well.
He reserves a special hug for James and Jim and tells them,
"Stay away from tombs and donkeys."

"What are you teaching next year?" Dina asks.

"Not sure, perhaps The Iliad."

"We'll be back next year," Brandon says. "That should be fun."

"I can't promise fun," Matthew responds, "but I can guarantee an epic adventure."

"Bye, Matthew," they say, waving and boarding the boat.

"Bye!" Matthew says. "Keep an eye out for Odysseus!"

For the first time he can remember, Matthew cannot concentrate on his work, so he decides to walk aimlessly about Mykonos. He finds himself once again at the Mykonos School for Dramatic Arts for Children. He stands quietly in the back of the School watching a group of children perform a traditional native dance, which he learns later is called *Kalamatianos*. Dancers appear to be dragging or pulling their feet as they move in a semicircle. It is a very festive number which usually opens celebrations.

Next, boys and girls assemble to play ancient instruments, but Matthew's attention is drawn to three boys who spontaneously break into a dance he has seen young children perform before. It is the *Hassapiko*, and the boys hold onto each other's shoulders as they dance, following the lead of the first in line, executing a few variations in step, but they always return to the same, rhythmic pattern.

Matthew enjoys watching the children dance, and it occurs to him that he knows of no other ethnic group where dance is so central to their lives. There seems to be a distinctive dance for each holiday and festival.

All of the children now assemble to sing of their country's glories. Ranging in age from six years to the early teens, the youngsters stand casually before the Master as they perform.

In the center is a curly-haired boy chosen to sing the solo part. His voice is that of an angel and his face, framed by a black crown of curls, is favored by the gods. As Matthew comes closer, he is sure he has seen the child somewhere, but where? Ah, It is the child Elena was painting, her godson, Nikos.

When the rehearsal ends, Grigoris greets Matthew and introduces him to Yiorgos, who is waiting to take Nikos home. He calls Nikos over to join them, introducing him as well.

"I am pleased to meet you," Matthew says and adds that, coincidentally, he knows Elena. He is surprised by Yiorgos' frozen look.

He then focuses all of his attention on the child, as good teachers do.

"Nikos, you have a fine, clear voice. Do you enjoy singing?"

"Yes, sir, I do."

"You enunciate very well—you must practice a good deal."

"Yes, sir, I do, but I enjoy it very much."

As they speak, Nikos feels special and becomes radiant.

"Matthew, let me introduce you to the other children," the Master says, explaining, "The younger children have been learning about 'Greece and the Sea' and the older ones have begun to read *The Odyssey*. I know they will be excited to tell you all about what they have learned."

Grigoris calls all the children to gather around and meet Matthew.

"Children, say hello to our guest, Mr. Wyttman. He is visiting here from Great Britain, and he also is a teacher."

"Καλημερα Κυριε Wyttman, Καλως ωρισατε στην Ελλαδα," (Goodday, Mr. Wyttman, welcome to Greece), the children say.

"Καλημερα παιδια, καλημερα!!" (Goodday, children, goodday!!), Matthew responds enthusiastically.

The children are excited about meeting a visitor, especially one who speaks their language. Although they see many tourists on Mykonos, it is rare for them to have an occasion to speak to one. Now that they are talking to Matthew, they call him "the stranger from across the sea."

Matthew is amused by this title, but from that day on, his friend, Grigoris, always calls him "the stranger from across the sea."

Matthew turns to the younger children and begins, "Now tell me..." but several of the children begin talking at once, in Greek, asking Matthew,

"How did you come here, by boat or airplane?"

"How far away is your home?"

"What do you teach?"

"Children, children," Grigoris says, assembling them in a circle around Matthew. "We speak to our guest one at a time. Besides, Mr. Wyttman has many questions to ask you."

"This young man is Gabriel," Grigoris tells Matthew, guiding an eight-year-old boy gently toward him.

"Gabriel, I'm pleased to meet you. What do you like best about school?"

"I like everything, sir, because I have much to learn," Gabriel says, then asks, "What is the name of the island where you live?"

"The island is called Great Britain, and the city where I live is London."

"And the sea—is the sea near London?"

The master interjects, "Remember what we learned in class, Gabriel, about the great river called Ocean?"

"Yes, sir," says Gabriel, "the great river called Ocean encircles the earth."

"Correct," Grigoris acknowledges.

"Excellent," adds Matthew. He begins to say, "Tell me about..." but the younger children, all very excited, ask:

"Do you like it there?"

"Is it very big?"

"Do you have a dog?"

Laughing, Matthew replies, "Yes, yes, and yes!!"

A young girl with large grey eyes, whose name is Athena, asks, "What is the name of your dog?"

"Argos, his name is Argos."

Alexis, one of the older boys, says, "Argos was the name of Odysseus' dog."

"That is correct," Matthew says. "Very good."

"Thank you, sir," Alexis says. "There is so much to learn from our great poet, Homer, but I just happened to remember the name of the dog because I like dogs."

Grigoris then explains that some of the older children have begun to recite *The Odyssey*.

"What kind of dog is Argos?" Athena, the grey-eyed child asks.

"He is a bulldog," Matthew replies.

"A bulldog!!" Alexis exclaims. "Is he half bull and half dog? Is he something like our Minotaur, half bull and half man?"

"No, he is all dog," Matthew explains, "but sometimes he has the personality of a bull!!"

Next, the Master introduces two young girls. "This is, Irini, one of our best dancers," he says, "and this is her sister, Angelica, another fine dancer."

Matthew says, "I have seen you dance, and you both are very talented. Do you practice every day?"

"Yes," the girls reply in unison and then ask Matthew, "Do you dance?"

"Do boys and girls dance where you live?"

"No and yes," Matthew says, laughing and turning to his friend. "Are the children always this curious?" he asks.

"Yes, they are," Grigoris responds. "They are filled with questions."

"This certainly is refreshing," Matthew says happily. "I'm touched by their innocence. They've shown me a different world."

"Yes," Grigoris cannot help but agree, "their world is special indeed."

Before he leaves, Matthew congratulates the children again and says kind and flattering words to Nikos.

Nikos asks plaintively, "Will you be our new teacher?"

Matthew is a bit startled and very softly he says, "No."

Nikos' heart hurts.

That evening, Claire arrives by plane, because she knows the *Penelope* takes more than four hours from Rafina and she cannot tolerate being confined that long on the boat. She bought a regular fare airline ticket from Athens to Mykonos, muttering that perhaps she should get a part-time job as a travel agent for free trips. She justifies the expense, however, because she has to talk to Matthew as soon as possible. Her major fear is that if Matthew does not get the Senior Lectureship, he will leave the university, possibly returning to his previous career as a writer and translator. She believes the sooner she can convince him of what he must do, the better.

"Do you know where Matthew Wyttman is?" she asks the manager of the Nissaki shortly after she arrives.

"He said he was going for a walk in town."

Matthew has chosen to walk through the famous maze in Mykonos, thinking that the labyrinthine ways match his emotions. He still cannot concentrate on his translations.

Claire travels these paths rapidly on sandals that seem to have wings, trying to find Matthew. Matthew is twisting and turning through the labyrinth as well. Neither knows the other is nearby, of course, and they keep missing one another as one makes a right turn and the other a left. Mykonos Town was built during Venetian times in the thirteenth century, and the maze was deliberately designed to confuse pirates and other invaders from the sea. Finally, Matthew sits at a taverna to sip a coffee, and Claire eventually finds him.

"I wonder if I should have ordered an ouzo," he mutters to himself as Claire joins him.

"I am so glad I found you," she says.

"It's rather easy to find someone here, just like following a string," he retorts.

Claire is breathless and flushed. Matthew is flushed, as well, but it is because he is flustered and disconcerted with Claire's intrusion into his life at this of all times. With great difficulty, he hides his feelings. In a rush, Claire explains the situation with the vote.

"You must return to persuade the promotions committee to recommend you," she declares. "Your presence is absolutely essential."

"Are you certain?" Matthew asks.

"Certain as certain can be. There has been a dramatic change in the situation. Until a few weeks ago, you were one of two contenders for this position."

"That's not the situation now?"

"No. Our colleagues became deadlocked in a trial vote and could not agree on which candidate should be selected.

They want to avoid causing a split amongst themselves and intend to go outside the department to hire a Senior Lecturer."

At this news, Matthew is clearly taken aback.

Claire says she has carefully analyzed the situation and knows which faculty members can be persuaded to change their votes and support him.

"If you truly want the Senior Lectureship, you must listen to me."

Reluctantly, Matthew listens. He has worked very hard for this prize. Perhaps he should return and meet privately with members of the committee and then contact some of the faculty members Claire says could be persuaded to support him.

"Claire, your reading of the situation is brilliant, I must agree."

"Matthew," she responds with laughter, "that is what I am all about—that is why I am called 'Claire,' French for brilliance!!"

He takes Claire to the Phillippi later that evening. It is one of the best restaurants on the island, noted for its excellent seafood. They are seated on the first floor in the garden. Other diners are on the balcony surrounding the garden. Between platters of grilled red mullet and side dishes of eggplant with tomato sauce and melted cheese, they discuss strategy.

Matthew wavers between being enthusiastic and sullen. The prize for which he has worked so hard may be his if he returns and lobbies for support. After listening to Claire, he is beginning to believe he can actually talk to his colleagues. He must return and build his case.

"It is unthinkable to bring an outsider into the department," Matthew says. "An impression will be created that we cannot solve our own problems."

"I agree, Matthew, I agree."

Matthew now sees clearly that Claire does have his best interests at heart. He has pierced beneath the veneer of her strong persona. Her personality, he believes, is defined by a spirit of generosity, and he sees this as a noble and honorable characteristic in a woman.

For the first time, he feels affection for her.

"Come, Claire, let me take you home," he says, placing a protective arm around her while walking to "Taxi" Square.

ᴙᴙᴙ

In the meantime, Elena is with her friends at the Vengera, a small bar frequented by the artists who spend the summer on Mykonos. They are writers, painters, and screenwriters, all talking excitedly about their projects. Elena, affronted by Matthew's rejection, flirts boldly and announces she is going dancing that evening at the Mykonos Bar. "Whoever wants to join me is welcome!" she declares.

A group of young people in ragged beach attire enters the Vengera. They say they are looking for anyone to help them prepare banners announcing the big Beach Party on Rhenia the next night. It will be the biggest party of the year, and the boats of all the fishermen have been reserved to take the partygoers to the island for a night of revelry.

"Everyone is welcome!!" the young people shout. "Come and join our party."

Everyone in the bar quickly gets into the mood and makes crudely lettered signs. As fast as they are lettered, the beach crowd scatters throughout the island and posts the announcements in every possible location.

Visitors who come to Mykonos regularly know that every summer in mid-July a spectacular party is held on Rhenia, much to the chagrin of Mykoniates who fish there or take animals to graze. The tourists must be catered to, however, and it is well known that a major reason an international mix of sophisticated partygoers converges on Mykonos in mid-July is because of this party, which some Mykoniates call a "Dionysian revelry."

ꙮꙮꙮ

The night before the revelry, Claire is in her room, rapidly and simultaneously packing, making phone calls to London, and ordering from room service. Elena is the center of attention at The Mykonos Bar, dancing non-stop with anyone who will join her. Matthew is walking in solitude on the beach, trying to sort out his feelings.

The clouds are unusually still as Sappho, Aphrodite, and Eros sleep soundly, empty goblets by their sides. But they awaken quickly when Hera arrives, causing the clouds to tremble. "Naughty nymphs," she says to the sleepy-eyed Sappho and Aphrodite, "you are a bad influence on this lovely young man, Eros, who never does wrong. But since you two have started your mischief with the mortals, you must finish it. Must I summon Zeus?" she asks, leaving as quickly as she arrived, and taking the remaining nectar with her.

Claire comes to Matthew's flat the next morning to ask if he wants to join her at the beach below.

"I have plans for the day and really can't spare the time."

"Oh, Matthew, relax a bit, will you?" Claire says in vexation. "My time here is short, and you and I have few opportunities to unwind together in such a beautiful setting as Mykonos."

"You're right. Sorry for being a bit stuffy."

"It's okay to deviate from form once in awhile, Matthew," Claire teases.

Matthew realizes she is becoming a valuable friend and colleague and reluctantly relents. To make amends, he says, "Since you're leaving tomorrow, why don't we spend the day on Kalo Livadi Beach? It is one of the most beautiful, secluded places on the island. I'd like to show it to you."

"I'll get my swimming costume."

"Brilliant," Matthew declares. "I'll arrange for a picnic lunch and a blanket, and we'll take a taxi there."

Before they depart, Matthew goes back to his flat to collect his things and pauses to arrange his manuscripts neatly. He moves the few pieces of china that the cleaning woman had placed on the table to the left side of the cupboard. Everything will be in its proper place tomorrow for afternoon tea.

ᄅᄅᄅ

There is no one within sight at the secluded spot on Kalo Livadi that Matthew has selected. They place the picnic lunch near them under the shade of a palm tree, but prefer to lie on a blanket under the rays of the sun.

"This is absolutely beautiful," Claire declares.

The island is indeed charming and, with the Aegean ebbing at their feet, the sea breezes fondling their slim torsos, and the whitest of clouds languishing above their heads, Matthew finds Claire charming, too. In this setting, alone at last with Matthew, Claire is radiating confidence and beauty. The brilliant sun creates deep red highlights in her auburn hair and causes her red bikini to sparkle. Claire sparkles. She flirts with Matthew in a charming way. Last night he showed her affection for the first time. Because of his new warmth toward her, and in the solitude of this spectacular setting, she believes this is a precious chance to take their relationship beyond friendship.

Matthew is feeling affection for Claire and tells her, "I'm truly grateful for your help. You have a very generous nature."

"Thank you, Matthew."

"I'm sincere. Your charm is your generosity."

"I would like to prove that point," Claire says as she leans toward Matthew and kisses him with the confidence of a mature woman. His senses have been so stimulated of late that he is instantly aroused.

Eros speeds onto the scene, bow and arrow ready, but Aphrodite sends him away, saying, "Not now, not now!!"

Lowering Claire to the blanket, Matthew turns to blend his body with hers, but rolls too far and is heavy on her. He straightens up a bit and begins kissing her passionately. Claire returns his kiss and to her it seems as though their very souls touch. Claire has never, ever been kissed like that.

Claire's kisses become fervent, deep, and burning. Matthew starts to cover her eyelids with kisses, but he misses and his lips rest on her nose. He starts to untie her halter-top, but fumbles and Claire removes the top herself, exposing her lovely, ample breasts for his pleasure.

The sun is directly overhead, white-hot and dead-still; warm steam appears to rise from the sand that is now a bright pink; and the gentle breeze which was a cool wisp moments earlier sticks to their bodies like a hot poker.

Claire cannot control the various sensations in her body, all of which are colliding simultaneously. The blood rushes to her face, her temples are pounding, and worst of all, her toes have begun to twitch! When Matthew's lips do begin exploring her body, her blistering thighs part in submission and moist anticipation.

Through parched lips, Claire moans, "Matthew, Matthew."

And then, suddenly, out of the clear blue sky there is a brilliant flash of light. It seems as though another presence is on the beach.

Seconds later a large beach ball comes bouncing past them, followed by a boy chasing it and crying, "Mother, Mother!"

Claire exclaims, "What in the..," but Matthew places his hand quickly over her mouth and fumbles about as he reassembles her bathing costume.

They are startled, but they move quickly to the shade of the palm tree and begin fussing over the picnic lunch because they know the mother will be close behind the intruding child. There is a sudden chill in the air. The sand is once again bleached white, not pink, and the breeze returns like a gentle fan.

Matthew says, "I am so sorry. How do you feel?"

Claire, covered with beads of sweat, sways toward Matthew and says there is a hum in her ears, her vision is blurred, she has totally lost her appetite, and she feels faint.

Matthew says "You do look a bit green," and he proceeds to gather their things and escort Claire to her hotel.

🔀🔀🔀

After a restless night, Claire prepares to leave and gathers her luggage. Matthew waits with her at the quay as she stands in line to board the *Penelope* for Athens. As they say goodbye, Claire says, "I plan to spend the night in Athens to catch a morning flight. I can be reached at the Athenian Inn if you would like to get in touch."

"Yes, I know the Athenian Inn. Lovely place in the Kolonaki section of Athens. I'll call you there."

They kiss goodbye, delighted in their mutual discovery of affection, thwarted though it was.

It's a perfect day for fishing, and the retired seafarers have finally convinced Tassos to go with them.

"Tassos—the saints bless you—you have finally come to your senses and set aside an afternoon for yourself," Stephanos declares.

"It is good to be with you again," Tassos says, adjusting the line resting on his index finger.

"I need to get away from town and all that talk about selling old property to make way for the new. 'A New Mykonos for the New Millennium, A New Mykonos for the New Millennium!!' My head spins."

"We know," says Nikolaos. "Our heads were spinning years ago."

"But you are happy now, right?" Tassos asks.

"I am happy when I am fishing," Petros says.

"Only then?" Tassos asks. "Only when you are fishing?"

"Tassos—the devil take my tongue if I lie to you—the money has not made me happy. It has made me secure, do not doubt that. My family will want for nothing!!"

"But?" Tassos asks.

"Ah, Tassos," Stephanos says, "we are not philosophers, we are simple men. We enjoy a simple life."

"Have you observed what is happening on our island?" Petros asks. "You don't have to sell your property to make money. If you are considering selling just to make money, you are doing it for the wrong reason."

"What do you mean?" Tassos asks.

"Let me tell him," Nikolaos says.

"Tassos," he begins, "you know the widow Sophia who has the farm behind the market, yes?"

"Yes."

"We see her going to the bank with shopping bags filled with *drachmas*!"

"Shopping bags filled with *drachmas*?"

"Yes."

"What is she doing? Selling lots of fruits and vegetables?"

"No," Nikolaos says, "—strike me now, St. Nikolaos, if I lie—she used to allow tourists to take her picture with her donkey and not charge them anything. Now she is charging 5,000 *drachmas* for one picture!"

"No!!" exclaims Tassos.

"Yes, yes," says Nikolaos.

"And that is just one example," Stephanos says. "Some men are taking the tourists on fishing trips to secret places that only they know, and the widows are selling handcrafted items as fast as they can make them. For many *drachmas*."

"Our way of life here has always been so simple," Nikolaos says. "It has taken awhile for people to understand how to be, what is the word, entrepreneurs?"

"You are a cobbler, Tassos," Petros teases. "Make sandals and carve the name of our island on the strap!!"

"Or invest your money wisely. The money you got when you sold your home by the beach—that is probably just in a savings account, right?" he asks.

"Yes, that is right."

"Well, if it is money you are worried about, there are so many opportunities for wise investments. Our relatives in Athens, the ones who now wear suits, could help you."

Tassos has much to think about. When he returns to his home, Katerina is waiting for him and he enters, saying, "Katerina, we must talk. Does your uncle still have that donkey?"

That afternoon, Matthew is once again wandering around Mykonos and cannot help but see the signs announcing the party. It seems that every fisherman has his boat by the quay, ready for passengers. Some of the boats are large enough to take a herd of sheep; some can hold only four passengers. Matthew remembers how enchanting this island is during the day and also during the evening storm. He decides to go with the crowd and see the island again on a clear night. He will remain aloof and observe the party.

⌐⌐⌐

When he arrives on Rhenia in the evening, most of the revelers are on the west side of the island, near the boats. There are huge bonfires blazing, creating a haunting and eerie atmosphere. Flames from the fires join with the enchanting light from hundreds of stars to bathe whirling dancers and rapturous revelers. Music from tapes popped into battery-operated radios pulsates. Couples wander from the crowd seeking private places away from the flickering flames, but under the magical starlight. It seems that everyone is drinking and the smell of marijuana is in the cool night air. Tonight, the island belongs to the god Dionysus.

It is not long before Matthew sees couples dancing vigorously to raucous rock music. He walks away from them toward the happy sound of Greek music and soon sees Elena dancing with girlfriends, as is the custom on Mykonos. They, however, are performing the *tsifte-teli*, a popular dance on the islands that has its roots in the East. It is lovely, lyrical, and sensual.

Elena and her two friends, Calypso and Antigone, are encircled by the artistic crowd from the Vengera, who watch respectfully and clap to the rhythm of the music. Matthew watches, unseen. In contrast to the other dancers who seem to be just moving about, Elena and her two friends are dancing slowly and erotically, taking great joy and delight in exhibiting their skill.

The scarlet flames from the fires cast shadows on the sands. The flames and shadows dance, like excited wizards, creating a spellbinding and bewitching stage for Elena and her enchanting friends. Matthew watches in stunned silence, transfixed by the splendor of the dance and the lyrical grace of the dancers.

Elena is the most inspired dancer of the trio. Matthew has seen her expressiveness during yoga, but now she is demonstrating her joy during a lovely dance while surrounded by flames and starlight. Matthew begins to feel weak—there is a humming in his ears, sweat is pouring from him, his vision becomes dim, and he begins to feel as though he is turning green!

Elena and her friends soon stop dancing and walk away from the crowd. Matthew moves to a higher spot so he can see them from above. They are animated and still filled with good cheer. Now they are engaged in the ritual of combing and braiding each other's hair after the vigorous dancing which causes them to perspire. A young woman stands behind Elena, combing her long hair and arranging it in braids. There is much laughter and gaiety, but to Matthew's eye, it is a sensual scene.

As Matthew watches, we hear his thoughts,

> "Closest to heaven is she
> who stands behind you,
> making braids of your hair."

The rational control he has always had over his emotions is ebbing away.

Suddenly, a man obviously intoxicated who was watching the women dance approaches them. "You, Elena, come dance with me," he says, waving a bottle. His behavior is raucous and obtrusive.

"Go away, go away," Elena says, but he continues to come toward her. Matthew rushes to Elena's side. Because the man is unsteady, it takes just a slight push from Matthew to unbalance him. Matthew takes a firm hold of Elena, and though she protests, he carries her away to the nearest boat, abducting her. He says to the boatman, "What is your name, sir?" The man answers, "Phaon."

"Phaon, really. Well, Phaon, please take us back to Mykonos."

"No, no, I want to stay," Elena says, "It is the biggest party of the year."

"This is no place for you, Elena," Matthew insists and tells the boatman to start the engines.

Matthew is in control and does not allow Elena to return to the island. As the boat leaves Rhenia, Elena is shouting at Matthew, "How dare you treat me this way?"

But Matthew is standing calmly and deliberately looking toward Mykonos with his back to the revelers. He mutters: "Barbarians. Lotus Eaters."

Knowing she cannot win, Elena stands quietly at the bow of the boat looking straight ahead. In the moonlight, Matthew sees her profile and it appears to be the boat's figurehead.

When the boat docks, Elena rushes away in a huff, ignoring Matthew's pleas to talk to him.

ᛞᛞᛞ

In Athens, Claire is warm with the afterglow of her intimate experience. She calls Matthew from The Athenian Inn to talk sweetly to him. But it seems she is talking to the old Matthew.

"Matthew, I am away from you just a short while, but I miss you so much."

"Ah, yes, it is just a bit ago that you popped over here."

Matthew remains polite and courteous, but is unresponsive to her words of endearment.

"Is something wrong?" she asks apprehensively.

"No, no," he says evasively.

"Matthew, I don't know what has happened in just a few days, but I really must talk to you. I'm coming back. This will surely take all my travel funds for the next few years, but I'll worry about that later."

She does not hear him demur, because she has rung off.

ᒧᒧᒧ

On the quay the next morning, Matthew sees Elena at a taverna talking excitedly to her mother and embracing her. When Katerina leaves, Elena finishes her coffee and reads newspapers her mother gave her. Matthew is about to approach Elena, but fears she is still upset with him. She is avidly reading the papers. He begins to walk away, hesitates, and stops at a spot near where Elena is sitting and asks a waiter to take a note to her. He writes in Greek,

> "Elena, only God could love you
> for yourself alone
> and not your silken hair."

It is not signed. Elena looks for Matthew, but he is confused by his feelings and hurries away, afraid of what her reaction might be.

Claire has now arrived at Mykonos and goes straight to Matthew's flat. He agrees they must talk, and they walk along the beach. Matthew had a difficult night. As they walk, he alternately embraces her and then becomes withdrawn. He appears about to make an announcement, but then does not. Claire is most solicitous and concerned and hesitates to talk about their intimacy on the beach. Instead, she picks a safe topic. She talks about the Senior Lectureship and reassures him that he is making the right decision.

In a torrent of words, Matthew says, "Claire, forgive me, for I'm so confused. I feel as though my world is unraveling. At this moment, the Senior Lectureship is the last thing on my mind."

"I have discovered magic," he declares passionately. "It exists on a primitive island where there are a few shepherds; it exists on a sacred island protected by the gods; it exists in the poetry of Sappho, and it exists in a dark-eyed goddess who is of the Aegean who has enchanted me with the kiss of Aphrodite.

"I cannot leave this island now," he says. "Perhaps never."

Claire is stunned, momentarily, into silence. Is this Matthew who spends his days and nights translating dead languages? Is this Matthew who has told her how much he enjoys his tea every day at 4 p.m.? Is this the man who was so generous in his affections? What has gone wrong? Claire delivers a tirade.

"I have lost my patience. You are foolish, irresponsible, and you really do not appreciate what I have been trying to do for you.

"Magic? Magic? You have been reduced, for God's sake, to babbling about the gods and poetry!!"

Claire knows she has lost any chance of captivating Matthew, so she continues to speak bluntly.

"Matthew," she says, "you say the Senior Lectureship is no longer important. And why? Because of magic, the gods, Sappho, and Aphrodite! For God's sake!!!

"You hold me in disdain for my attempts to relate in a personal way to the literature we both love. Now your very life has become a personal response!!

"Matthew, I said your life has become a personal response!!!"

She has a parting shot: "Really, Matthew, I didn't think you could make a commitment to anything beyond the fifth century B.C."

Claire says she will spend this evening on the island and return the next morning by plane to Athens and then on to

London. "To hell with my bloody travel budget!!" she says. "If you change your mind, you can find me at the Hotel Pestino here or call me in London."

◪◪◪

When Matthew finds Grigoris that afternoon, school is over and he is preparing to go fishing. It is obvious to Grigoris that Matthew is distraught; he has never seen him so confused.

"My friend," the Master says, "come, let us talk." They walk to the marina and sit in his small boat.

"Are you going fishing, Grigoris?"

"Yes, but just for awhile. I must return well before dark because I am getting older, you know, and my sight is beginning to fade."

"Grigoris," Matthew begins, "to me, you will always be ageless. But dear friend, I have some questions of you."

"I am always here for you. Ask your questions."

"If Odysseus had acknowledged the power of the gods, he would have found his way home straight away, don't you agree?"

Startled by this strange question, Grigoris replies, "Well of course, but the whole point..."

Matthew interrupts his friend. "Things were out of his control, right?" he persists.

"Well, yes—and—"

"If Odysseus had shown more respect for the gods, he may have had a safer journey, do you agree?"

"My friend..."

"He fought against tremendous odds, did he not?"

"But of course..."

But again, Matthew interrupts.

Suddenly changing the subject, Matthew asks, "I say, my friend, are you happy teaching the children? Do you miss teaching at university? Do you miss your colleagues?"

The Master tells him he is happy teaching the children. "No, I do not miss teaching at university," he says emphatically.

"What about your colleagues, your associates? Do you miss them?"

"My colleagues are the children."

"And your associates?"

"My associates are the children."

"I am learning much from them," Grigoris adds, underscoring his point.

Hearing this, Matthew falls silent.

"But they are so innocent," he says finally, very quietly.

"Yes," Grigoris replies.

"They are filled with questions," Matthew whispers.

"Yes," Grigoris agrees.

"They represent another world," Matthew fumbles.

"They do," his friend affirms.

"When they are happy, they break into dance!"

"Yes, they do!!"

He falls silent again. Rising, he takes Grigoris' hand.

"You once called me 'the stranger from across the sea.' I want to be your friend," he says bending to kiss him Greek style, first on one cheek, then on the other.

"You are my friend," Grigoris replies, "my dear friend."

"Ευχαριστω πολυ," (Thank you very much) Matthew says, embracing Grigoris.

"Παρακαλω," (You are welcome) Grigoris replies, returning his friend's embrace.

The newspapers Elena read so avidly contained two stories that stunned her. One was of the raucous party. Because of the tourist trade, the papers usually did not write pointed criticism of this event. There was an incident, however. One of the revelers had grabbed a gun from a man who had been grazing his sheep on the island and inadvertently shot another tourist. The tourist had been flown to Athens; the full extent of his injuries was not known.

The second story was presented from different points of view in the opposing newspapers and gave the latest news on the development plans.

One headline read:

ROMANTIC IDEALISTS SUCCEED:
PROGRESS STOPPED FOR MYKONOS

The other headline read:

WINDMILLS SAVED!!!
DEVELOPERS DEFEATED

Each newspaper told its version of the story about how the development plan was defeated because key residents decided not to sell their land for the marina and the airport. One family who was now refusing to sell was Tassos and Katerina Angelides.

Elena is elated that her parents will not sell their land and finally understand her point of view. But she is shamed by the story of the tragedy at the party. What direction should her life take now? How can she be two people? The Elena who likes to party and be so free that she denies her family, culture, and religion? The Elena whose soul was so touched by lyric poetry that it makes her see with new eyes and feel with new senses? She remembers the phrase from her classes in ancient Greek, "on the one hand, on the other hand." Is she two people? Perhaps Matthew was right to carry her away from the party, but she didn't like it.

ᛡᛡᛡ

Elena walks slowly along the beach where she normally practices her *asanas*, but she cannot do her practice because she is depressed. As she moves along the beach, she comes upon a woman and two children playing on the edge of the sea. Both children are boys. One is about five or six years of age, the other a toddler who has just learned to walk. She assumes the woman is the mother of the boys.

Elena pauses to meditate and reflect upon the decisions she has made in her young life. She loves her parents, but she feels their expectations are unrealistic. Their religion and culture are central to their lives, and they desire that

PAN   SAPPHO   THE THREE   GRACES

Elena share these loves. Her mother visits her church as
often as she can, tenderly kissing the icons. Her father contributes articles on Greek culture to the local newspapers
and is constantly reading about the ancient world and partic-
ipating in cultural preservation projects. Elena respects her
religion and culture, but she expresses her love differently.

As Elena reflects, she watches the young mother and her
two children. The mother sits with her back to Elena on a
large blanket, holding her youngest while the older, curly-
haired boy is between her feet playing in the sand. For several minutes, she playfully lifts the toddler high above her
head, gently rocking him to and fro, then kisses his forehead as she lowers and embraces him. After each embrace,
she then reaches for her older son and tickles his feet.
Happy, joyous sounds come from the boys. Both are
delighted with this game. The mother soon lowers the
infant and places him gently by her side. Spontaneously,
the older boy runs to his mother to kiss her.

As Elena's gaze is fixed on the mother's back, she sees just the top of the child's dark, curly hair and watches as his small hands circle his mother's neck in a tender embrace. Elena's heart hurts.

She rushes to the home of a friend to borrow books on Sappho, then returns to her flat. Elena has not read Sappho since high school and has just one of her books. After a careful reading, she begins to complete the work she had begun on three watercolors. She signs all three paintings Ελενη and writes short poems on each one. She takes one to her parents' home, but they are not there, and she leaves it, planning to return later.

ᘃᘃᘃ

Matthew is struggling with feelings that are very disturbing to him. Should he return to London and attempt to salvage the promotion he covets? Should he pursue Elena? Matthew feels confused, as though he is back in the maze. He feels as though he is between two worlds. He leaves his flat; perhaps he will visit Delos again, perhaps not.

D awn is just breaking as Elena rushes to Matthew's flat; he is not there; she leaves two paintings with the hotel manager. She then goes to her parents' home, bearing gifts of kalamata olives, fresh tomatoes, and cucumbers.

As Elena enters, her Mother exclaims, "Καλημερα, Ελενη μου, καλως ωρισες στο σπιτι!!" (Good morning, my Elena, welcome home!!)

"Καλημερα καλημερα, μητερα μου." (Good morning, good morning, my mother.)

As they embrace, Elena notices that they have uncovered the painting.

The painting is of Nikos and signed,

"For my son, Nikos, from your Mother, Elena."

A poem is written in the left-hand corner. Elena, her parents, and Yiorgos have an emotional reconciliation. Elena seeks their forgiveness and attempts to explain her past behavior. She speaks in her native tongue:

> My golden, childhood memories
>   dwell in a dark house.
> I have no gift of a seaside feast to give to
>   my honey-voiced son.
> I live with pain that never sleeps.
> Misguided, I bowed at the altar of the god
>   Dionysus.
> Cursed by the gods, I can look neither
>   backward nor forward.
> Shame's black-tattered robe now covers me.

Her parents respond:

> We forgive you, as we ask you to forgive us.
> On our shoulders rests the blame for your
>   sorrows.
> In our hearts lies your pain, falling drop by
>   drop.
> House of Somnus, ancient House of Sleep,
>   open wide your doors; enter pain and
>   sorrow.
> Ελενη, throw off your black-tattered robe.
> Ελενη, come home, come home!!

Ελενη comes home.

"I cannot go through life without experiencing motherhood and the joy of nurturing my child," she says. "I was wrong to deny this part of my life. I want to rear my son."

She says Nikos' father can live in Northern Greece, but she will remain here.

Her parents are overjoyed.

"Where is Nikos?" she asks.

"He is sleeping in the next room," her mother says.

Elena says soon she will hear Nikos sing and she herself will entertain them with readings of lyric poetry!

There is much embracing and kissing. Elena's mother holds her in a firm embrace and does not want to release her.

"I must see Nikos now, if only for a moment," Elena declares.

"Go to him," Katerina says.

The boy is asleep on his bed. Golden-sandaled dawn is tiptoeing into the room.

Elena kneels beside Nikos' bed, whispering softly, "Forgive me. I love you, my precious one.

"Our famous poet, Sappho, wrote a song for her beloved daughter, Cleis. I now offer this poem for you. Someday I will teach it to you." She whispers softly:

> Sleep, my dear
> I have a darling son Nikos,
> who is like a golden flower;
> I would not exchange him
> for the opulence of Lydia
> nor the charm of [Lesbos].

Immortal Dawn stands behind Elena as she rises and gently covers her mortal daughter with a gossamer, ruby-hued robe.

Sappho is so touched she begins to weep. Truly, her words will live forever!! She must reward Matthew and Elena. She calls to Aphrodite, who is walking about, scattering stardust in her path, and says "Come, golden-throned sister, we must visit the mortals."

Claire is in her flat with Argos by her side. She is knitting Matthew's scarf and has called him several times, but he has not been available. Finally, she calls again; this time Matthew is in his flat and is called to the telephone.

She says, "I am truly sorry to tell you that something has gone horribly wrong with the Senior Lectureship. Please believe me when I tell you I lobbied for you. I am sure it would have been different had you been here."

"Claire—" Matthew begins.

But Claire says, "please let me finish. I canvassed the faculty, mostly by telephone. At first, they were completely confused about what they were going to be asked to vote on come the fall semester. I spent a lot of time talking to each one individually. Apparently, so did members of the promotions committee!!! Anyway, it seemed to me they were evenly split. We needed one vote to ensure it for you and I tried to reach Pennypacker."

"He was headed for Egypt last time I talked to him."

"He is still there and cannot be reached by phone."

"Probably working on the hieroglyphics."

"No, he is meditating in the King's Chamber, stretched out in the sarcophagus of the Spinx trying to connect with new spiritual horizons. Left strict instructions that he is not to be disturbed."

"Are you serious?"

"Yes. He called me before going into the King's Chamber. He was going on and on about a new idea that suddenly came over him. He said buried under the Sphinx could be the lost Hall of Records from Atlantis. Pennypacker said someone has to take the lead if they are ever to be found."

"He is looking for lost records from Atlantis?"

"Yes. He thinks they are there and have just gone missing. Matthew, Matthew, are you there?"

"Yes, I'm here. A sinking feeling has just come over me," Matthew sighs.

"In any event, Matthew, I could not reach Pennypacker and while I was trying to do so, our colleagues changed their minds again."

"I'm getting dizzy."

"I may as well tell you straight away."

"Please do."

"They felt there was no alternative but to go outside the department. It seems clear this is what they will do in September. They agree on one thing only. They want to give the Senior Lectureship to a Postmodern scholar who champions the use of the personal voice in scholarship. I cautioned them that becoming personally involved with one's subject does have its dangers. I'm sure they thought I was being 'witty.'"

"What did you say?"

"I told them that under certain circumstances becoming involved with the 'personal voice' could well change one's life!

"Right, Matthew?" she asks. "Can't it change one's life?"

"I am sure I don't know what you mean."

"Will you return here anyway?"

"I'm of two minds—I feel as though my world is unraveling."

"You probably won't return."

"Probably not."

"May I please keep Argos?"

"It saddens my heart to lose him, but yes, you may keep Argos."

Claire wishes him the best, but says she must ring off now because the dog is nearby, staring at her as if he can hear their conversation. She explains, "He's giving strong signs that he wants to go out so I had better take him to the park before 'my pup runneth over!!'"

Matthew is most happy to end their conversation with humor, and they ring off.

Claire's emotions are a bit overwhelming; she hurries to get the dog's leash because she wants to escape to the park. As she searches for the leash, Argos growls, then runs happily through the living room with the yarn in his mouth, methodically unraveling the scarf Claire has been patiently knitting for Matthew.

At the Hotel Akrogiali, Yannis sits at a corner table and is deep in conversation with an older Greek woman whose face is expertly made up and hair is expertly coiffured. She is dressed very fashionably in expensive clothing. Her gold earrings, necklace, and bracelet are very bold and distinctive. She is propositioning Yannis.

"You can be the maître d', head waiter, or even the manager. My hotel is centrally located in Castoria and is open year round. You will not have to spend your summers in Mykonos. I will pay you what you are worth.

"My clientele will love you. Your personality is so Greek, so warm. Each evening we feature Greek dancing. I hear you are an excellent dancer. You can entertain my guests and do a dance whenever the mood strikes you!! You will be a star!!

"You have so many talents, you can have a good life at my hotel. And we are close to small villages if you want to escape.

"Most of all, you will be happy!!"

To Yannis' mind, she is offering him the world. It will be everything he wants. It will be paradise.

Yannis says, "You have overwhelmed me. What can I possibly give you in return for this golden opportunity?"

The woman stares straight into his eyes and says: "The recipe for lobster and spaghetti!!"

"Agreed," says Yannis.

Elena spends the rest of the day wandering around Mykonos looking for Matthew and finally takes the boat to Delos in search of him; she stands before Mt. Kynthos, debating whether she should make the climb. She climbs as rapidly as she can to the top, looks everywhere, goes into the cave, but he is not there. She returns, goes to his flat, and discovers that he has left the island. She is crestfallen and walks slowly away.

Meanwhile, Matthew is on the *Penelope* headed for Athens with a stop at Tinos. He is going to return to London. Yes. But thoughts of magic, the gods, Sappho, the dark-eyed goddess of the Aegean, and the kiss of Aphrodite are making his heart pound and his ears hum. Should he return to London? No. The boat stops at Tinos. He disembarks, stands on the shore, and walks through the small town to the opposite shore.

The beach is isolated, and Matthew walks slowly along the water's edge, reflecting. He is between the horns. Each foot is in a different hemisphere. He is still of two minds.

Feeling the need to stretch and release all the tension from his body, Matthew stops, rolls his shoulders back, rolls his neck, and lets his arms hang limply by his side. Then, in one long stretch, he raises his arms high above his head, bends forward, and effortlessly touches his face to his knees!

Matthew feels liberated. He rushes back through the town to take the hydrofoil back to Mykonos. But as he hurries past a hall, he hears the sound of a choir of women singing. Their songs are haunting and tantalizing. He is paralyzed by the music and cannot move.

Sappho and Aphrodite are watching over Matthew. When they hear the sirens, they summon Aeolus immediately. Within minutes, a wind swirls around Matthew, blocking his ears.

He moves quickly, racing to the hydrofoil.

He will return to Mykonos. YES. Now, at last, he is of one mind. The rapid hydrofoil, the *Delphini*, speeds him back to Mykonos, away from the haunting music. Going directly to his flat, Matthew finds the paintings from Elena.

Honey-voiced Sappho and violet-robed Aphrodite watch with pleasure from above and send a gentle breeze to take the cover from the first painting.

It is of a beautiful, golden-sandaled creature standing near the bedside of a sleeping woman.

It is signed, "με Αγαπη Ελενη και Σαπφω." (With Love, Elena and Sappho.)

The line on the painting reads:

> Suddenly,
> at my bedside
> stands golden-sandaled Dawn.

Matthew is enthralled.

Before he can remove the cover from the second painting, a gentle breeze lifts it.

This painting depicts a nearly barren tree with a lone red apple atop. A hand reaches high to grasp the lone apple.

It is signed, in Greek,

"Φτανω οσο πιο ψηλα μπορω, Ελενη." (I am reaching as high as I can, Elena.)

Matthew reads the poem Elena has written on the painting. Written in Greek, the poem reads:

> You are to me a lone red apple,
> high atop the tallest tree.
> Some say all who came
> passed it by; I say none
> could reach that high.

Matthew must find Elena. He now knows that through her, he will discover himself. He rushes and rents a moped!! First he goes to the Mykonos School in search of his friend, Grigoris.

"Is the teaching job still open, and do you still want me?"

"Yes, yes!"

Next, he goes in search of Elena at the quay and cannot find her. If he cannot be with her now, he will return to the top of Mt. Kynthos where they spent that magic night. If he cannot find her, he will surely die!! And if he must die, he will die on that mountain. Or perhaps he will make the

Leucadian leap! If he can, he will ride the moped to the top of Mt. Kynthos!

As quickly as possible, he goes to Delos and climbs Mt. Kynthos. There in solitude, on the sacred island, Elena is practicing her *asanas*. He watches her for some time. When she executes her backward bend, he approaches her. As she comes three-quarters of the way up from this graceful posture, he rushes toward her. Embracing her, he implores, "Elena, teach me to dance."

ΤΕΛΟΣ
(The End)

THE MUSES

RECIPE
FOR
LOBSTER AND SPAGHETTI

For this recipe to be as good as the Lobster and Spaghetti served at the famous Hotel Akrogiali, everything must be fresh!!

INGREDIENTS
Kalamata olive oil
One onion from the garden
Two carrots from the garden
Garlic from the garden
6 to 8 tomatoes from the garden
Basil from the garden
Lemon from the tree
Lobster from the sea

MARINARA SAUCE
Heat olive oil in a pan and sauté onion and carrot until very soft. Put through food mill and set aside. Saute three cloves of garlic in the same pan, then add tomatoes, basil, salt and pepper, and the onion and carrot mixture. Simmer 15 minutes.

LOBSTER
Put the lobster in boiling water for 10 seconds. Remove and split lobster in half. Spread butter and olive oil over lobster and broil until done, about 10 to 15 minutes, depending upon size of lobster. Remove tail and place lobster meat from the tail on top of the steaming lobster. Place cooked spaghetti in the lobster shell, cover with marinara sauce. ENJOY!

IT IS THE BEST!!!!!!!!!!!

SAPPHO

Sappho is an ancient Greek lyric poet about whom we actually know very little. She lived on the island of Lesbos in the seventh and sixth centuries B.C., and her skills were praised by ancient writers. Her genius was the creation of a unique meter, called the Sapphic meter, very difficult to reproduce in English. The poet, Horace, paid her the supreme compliment by imitating this meter and the unique structure of her odes.

Sappho was born in either Mitylene or Eresus on Lesbos. She lived at a time of intellectual richness along the coast of Asia Minor near great cultural centers such as Ephesus, Smyrna, and Phocaea.

The renowned classics scholar, C.M. Bowra, speculated that Sappho was the leader of the cult of Aphrodite which trained young girls in various arts. He points out that Sappho herself refers to a μοισοπολονδομος (a house that cultivates the muses). Other scholars dispute this view. Professor Denys L. Page, for example, says Sappho's poetry simply represents the everyday loves and jealousies of the poet and her companions.

Mary Barnard, in her book, *Sappho*, points out that in sixth century Greece, young women were encouraged to study poetry and music, and that they sang and danced at festivals in honor of Artemis and Aphrodite. She adds that the songs in some religious exercises were performed exclusively for and by women. Ms. Barnard finds it plausible, therefore, that mothers would send their daughters to be trained by the most famous lyricist of the age.

While it is fascinating to speculate on Sappho's life, it is a supreme joy to read the poems and fragments that have survived from the nine books of poetry that we know she wrote. The poems are beautiful, and it is most interesting to see how various scholars translate these poems.

Two excellent translations are Mary Barnard's *Sappho*, and Margaret Williamson's *Sappho's Immortal Daughters.*

GREEK DANCING

There is a saying that it is impossible to separate the dancer from the dance; this is especially true of Greek dancing. Although there are hundreds of dances, each represents a specific emotion or is performed for a specific occasion. Yvonne Hunt, an expert in this area, explains that the dances are living expressions of a whole range of emotions, including heroism, courage, patriotism, and self-sacrifice, as well as expressions of love, hope, and happiness.

References to dancing are found in ancient literature. Plato said a man who cannot dance is uneducated and unrefined, and added that an accomplished dancer is the epitome of a cultured man. The ancients used just one word, ορχεσις, which means dance, music, and song, to describe dance.

Ms. Hunt explains that dancing is an ancient form of community entertainment that holds true today. "These dances cannot be separated from the everyday life of the Greeks for it is within the context of their lives that the dances have meaning," she explains and cites historical, national, social, religious, and cultural events in the yearly calendar of music and dancing.

In her book, *Traditional Dance in Greek Culture*, Ms. Hunt says: "The dances of Greece are so many and varied that it is difficult to try to classify or group them. However, they do tend to have regional similarities and can be classified in such broad categories as mainland, island, plains, mountain, and urban dances. Each of these groups has its own characteristics which are thought by some to reflect their particular geographical traits: the tall, majestic mountains are evident in the stately, proud bearing of the local inhabitants of mountainous villages as they move with simple steps combined with high lifts and leaps (for the men); dances of the plains regions seem to be more "earthy" with running steps, stamping, and lifts not so far from the ground. Islanders tend to move in a way which reminds one of the sea, as their dances seem to flow and undulate in a lifting manner reminiscent of the waves."

Ms. Hunt says in modern Greece the dance is associated with activities of the Greek Orthodox Church and is not to be overlooked nor taken lightly. She said dance occurs during celebrations either in or under the sponsorship of the church, and this religious association appears to date as far back as Minoan times.

It was the film *Zorba the Greek*, from the novel by Nikos Kazantzakis, that introduced non-Greeks to Greek dancing with all its passions and relevance to life. In the words of Zorba, "to live is to dance, to dance is to live." Long live Greek dancing!!

HISTORY OF THE PUB QUIZ

There is no definitive account of where or how the Pub Quiz came about, but it probably stems back to the early days of television game shows.

The pub was usually the place where people socialized, plus it probably had a television set before many of the homes.

There is always somebody who knows something about any subject under the sun, so any quiz show that was on television naturally drew attention. People would often be heard shouting out the answers before the studio contestants. Calls of "Why don't you go on that show?" would be heard. Bar owners are always quick to spot an opening—if you notice, quizzes are normally held on slack nights—and were happy to draw in punters for another evening. Teams always bring supporters, so the idea of local leagues, adding competition, would have appealed.

The first league I took part in to raise money for local charities would have been 1974. There were over thirty teams from different pubs in the district. It was divided up into four league areas, and there were home and away leagues with two points being awarded for a win. The leaders from each section went through to the knock-out stage, and the winners of the whole competition received trophies and were naturally well-treated by the owner of the pub they represented.

Local charities did well, also. The quiz was always held on a Monday, Tuesday, or Wednesday night, so if your team wasn't competing, you would go to speculate at another match, partly to look at the opposition, plus perhaps pick up more answers to trivia questions.

The only people who really had to work hard were the compilers of the quiz.

The BBC had a television show in the 1970s called "Master Team." For the first three series it was always won by teams from Northern Ireland. This is probably due to the fact that at that time the political situation there was so bad with sectarian murders at a high level. People would stay at home reading up on trivia amongst other things, rather than risk going out during dark winter nights.

By Finbar Fleming
Reprinted with his permission

Liam McAtasney, editor of "Brainstormer News," a newsletter devoted to the Pub Quiz, estimates that more than 400,000 people representing 6,000 pubs in Ireland and Britain participate in quiz nights on a regular basis. He says it has been slow to catch on in the United States, but about a dozen bars in both Boston and San Francisco hold weekly quizzes.

BILL PAPAS—ILLUSTRATOR

A Lone Red Apple was illustrated by Bill Papas. During the sixties, Bill Papas was the political cartoonist for *The Guardian, Sunday Times*, and *Punch Magazine* in London. At the same time he wrote and illustrated innumerable children's books for Oxford University Press, several of which had Greek themes, as well as illustrating books by such luminaries as C.S. Lewis, Pope John Paul I, and Malcom Muggeridge for Collins Publishers.

Bill and his wife Tessa met in London at that time, married, and moved to Ermioni, the village Bill's father had left sixty years previously. They spent the next thirteen years sailing the Aegean and Ionian seas on their yacht in the summer and living in the village during the winter months.

Bill continued to write and illustrate books and give exhibitions in Athens. In 1979 they were invited by the Jerusalem Foundation to stay in Jerusalem for six months. The result of this sojourn was a collaborative effort entitled *People of Old Jerusalem*, which was published in 1980.

Bill and Tessa left Greece in 1983, lived briefly in Switzerland, and then moved to Portland, Oregon. The most recent book produced by Bill and Tessa is *Papas' Greece*, a beautifully illustrated book that is an affectionate and humorous look at life in Greece during the seventies.

Aurelia is a student of the classics, a Philhellene, and a 1974 graduate of Duquesne University. She lives in Pittsburgh, Pennsylvania, and writes for *Greek America* magazine. For the past fifteen years she has lived in London during the summer months and during recent summers she lived also in Athens and Mykonos. Her novel is a result of her experiences living abroad. She is married to Dr. John W. Smeltz, retired from the English faculty at Duquesne University. This is her first novel. Aurelia calls *A Lone Red Apple* "My love song to Sappho and valentine to Greece."